"Obey me, and..."
everyone. Especially your...

Obey him?

Th_ _as what had gotten her into this trouble
in _e first place. Just off Copacabana Beach, to
th_ rhythmic beat of samba music and the howls
o_ the crowds, he'd looked back at her. He'd
t_ _en her in his arms and kissed her with a sud-
d_n ferocity that had made her weak. "You're
c_ming home with me," he'd whispered against
t_e flushed heat of her skin. "You're coming to
m_y bed..."

A_d she hadn't resisted. She'd thought she was
i_ love with him. She'd dreamed so long of
b_ _ng his, and she'd surrendered to his orders
v_thout a fight.

B_t back then she'd only risked herself. Now
s__ was pregnant. Her baby had to be protected
a_ _ll costs. If Diogo meant her harm....

"_ou said you didn't want to be a father. I ac-
ce_t that." She shook her head desperately.
"S_nd me back home. We'll never bother you
ag_n. The child will never even know about
y_ _."

Di_go's dark eyebrows lowered. "Because you
have other plans? No," he said with a curl on
his lip. "No baby of mine will leave Rio."

Jennie Lucas grew up dreaming about faraway lands. At fifteen, hungry for experience beyond the borders of her small Idaho city, she went to a Connecticut boarding school on scholarship. She took her first solo trip to Europe at sixteen, then put off college and travelled around the US, supporting herself with jobs as diverse as gas station cashier and newspaper advertising assistant. At twenty-two she met the man who would be her husband. After their marriage, she graduated from Kent State with a degree in English. Seven years after she started writing she got the magical call from London that turned her into a published author.

Since then life has been hectic, with a new writing career and a sexy husband and two babies under two, but she's having a wonderful (albeit sleepless) time. She loves immersing herself in dramatic, glamorous, passionate stories. Maybe she can't physically travel to Morocco or Spain right now, but for a few hours a day, while her children are sleeping, she can be there in her books.

Jennie loves to hear from her readers. You can visit her website at www.jennielucas.com, or drop her a note at jennie@jennielucas.com

VIRGIN MISTRESS, SCANDALOUS LOVE-CHILD

BY
JENNIE LUCAS

MILLS & BOON

Pure reading pleasure™

First published in Great Britain 2009
Harlequin Mills & Boon Limited,
Eton House, 18-24 Paradise Road, Richmond, Surrey TW9 1SR

© Jennie Lucas 2009

ISBN: 978 0 263 87008 4

Set in Times Roman 10½ on 12¼ pt
01-0309-43080

Printed and bound in Spain
by Litografia Rosés, S.A., Barcelona

VIRGIN MISTRESS, SCANDALOUS LOVE-CHILD

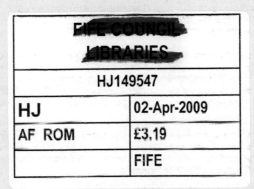

To Pete, who offered to whisk me to Rio for "research". Happy anniversary, honey, today and forever.

CHAPTER ONE

PREGNANT.

As Ellie Jensen came up the stairs from the subway, her body was still shaking. She dimly heard taxi drivers yelling curses and honking their horns. Vendors were already setting up hot dog and pretzel carts on the sidewalks. After a long, gray winter, New York had finally surrendered to the brilliant warmth of May.

But Ellie was cold to the bone. She hadn't felt her fingers or toes for hours. Not since she took the pregnancy test that morning and saw those two parallel pink lines

Pregnant.

She was getting married in six hours, and she was pregnant.

With another man's baby.

Her *boss's* baby.

Ellie stopped dead in front of the Serrador Building. She craned her neck to look up at the thirtieth floor, and panic ripped through her.

Diogo Serrador, the dark, ruthless steel tycoon who'd employed her for the last year, was going to be a father.

I cannot get you pregnant, querida. She still remembered his sensual voice that hot night, riding the hot drumbeat of Rio's *Carnaval*. He'd whispered against her skin, *Do not worry. It's impossible.*

And she'd believed him!

How could she have been so stupid? With her history, how could she have fallen prey to the oldest cliché in the world—an innocent country girl moving to the big, bad city and getting seduced by her arrogant, wealthy, vastly sexy boss?

She should have left the company at Christmas, when Timothy did. At the very least, she should have given notice weeks ago—as she'd promised him she would. But she'd kept procrastinating. As if something would stop her from losing the city she loved. The life she loved. The man she…

She stopped the thought cold.

It had been just a crush. A wild, heart-pounding crush. Then a seduction…

Ellie's heart hurt as she looked up at the brilliant blue sky above the sweetly singing birds. The air was fresh and warm. The world was new.

But the news of her pregnancy wouldn't make Diogo a father. She knew that already. The notorious playboy had his choice of gorgeous, brilliant women. He took them out, treated them like goddesses, then discarded them like last night's rubbish. If women like that couldn't hold his attention, no wonder he'd forgotten Ellie, a high school dropout with cheap clothes and unremarkable looks!

Diogo Serrador, a decent father?

The most likely scenario was that he'd carelessly offer her money for an abortion.

"Oh…" Covering her face with her hands, she cursed him aloud, causing the pedestrians hurrying past her on the sidewalk to give her a wide berth.

As inconvenient a shock as this pregnancy was, Ellie had already come to love this baby ferociously. This child was hers. *Her family*.

But Diogo had the right to know. Didn't he?

Ellie ground her teeth. She would fling his lie back into his face!

She pushed open the building's wide revolving door and took the elevator to the thirtieth floor. Determination steeled her as she passed the glassed-in offices down the hall.

"You're late," Carmen Alvarez snapped at Ellie as she passed her desk. "The numbers you gave me last night were all wrong. What's the matter with you, girl?"

Ellie felt the floor move beneath her in a sway of nausea. She'd nearly been sick twice on the subway ride from her tiny Washington Heights studio apartment. She'd been queasy for months. That should have warned her, but she'd told herself her cycle was erratic. She couldn't be pregnant. Diogo Serrador had given his word! *I cannot get you pregnant,* querida.

"Are you sick?" Mrs. Alvarez demanded with narrowed eyes. "Partying all night?"

"Party?" Ellie gave a weak laugh. That morning, when she'd finally been unable to zip up the black pencil skirt or button her close-fitting white shirt, she'd gone to the twenty-four-hour drugstore and bought a test from the pimply-faced teenager at the cash register. "No, not a party."

"Then it's some man," the older woman said. "I've seen this before. Wait right there." Holding up her finger in warning, the executive secretary answered the phone. "Diogo Serrador's office," she chirped brightly, turning away.

One of the other junior secretaries crept up to pat Ellie's shoulder.

"Did you see Mr. Serrador's picture in the papers this morning?" Jessica said in a sweet Southern drawl. "He took Lady Allegra Woodville to the benefit last night. She's so elegant and beautiful, don't you think? But then she comes from an upper-class background, just like he does. Blood will tell, my mama always used to say, class—" she looked over Ellie with hard eyes "—or trash."

Ellie ground her teeth. She never should have confessed her infatuation for Diogo—or her heartache after Rio.

Jessica saw her job simply as a way to pass the time until she found a rich husband, and she'd long ago set her sights on Diogo. Ellie had been trying to warn the girl with her own heartbreak.

Instead, Jessica had spread malicious rumors all over the office. Ellie was now despised by all the staff as a gold-digging slut. Ellie—a slut! She, who'd never even kissed a man before. Diogo had swept her up into his arms in Rio!

Thank God she'd finally given up on her dreams. She'd finally realized that her grandmother was right.

Her heart wasn't hard or modern enough to survive city life. She'd given up. *Given in.*

Three weeks ago, she'd finally told Timothy yes.

He had left his prestigious job as Diogo Serrador's general counsel at Christmas, abruptly deciding to be a simple country lawyer in their small hometown. He'd pressured Ellie to leave with him, but she'd refused.

But after today she would never have to see New York again—or Diogo. She would be married to a safe, respectable man who loved her. A man she could trust.

Assuming Timothy still wanted her when she was pregnant with another man's child.

Mrs. Alvarez hung up the phone and turned to face Ellie. "I don't know what you've been doing in your spare time, but your work has been unacceptable. This is your last chance—"

Diogo's deep, accented voice interrupted her, booming through the intercom on the elegant dark wood desk. "Mrs. Alvarez, come at once."

A thrill of panic raced through Ellie at the sound of his voice, causing her heart to nearly leap out of her chest.

"Yes, sir," the executive secretary replied, then released the intercom button. Her critical eyes traced over Ellie's pale, sweaty face and shapeless dark dress. "I need you to create a new SWOT analysis on Changchun Steel in dollars." When Ellie didn't move, she said sharply, "Get going, girl."

"No," Ellie whispered.

Mrs. Alvarez turned back with surprise and anger in her eyes. "What did you say?"

Shaking but determined, Ellie faced down the older woman. "I need to see him."

She looked dumbfounded. "Certainly not!"

"Let her go," Jessica muttered under her breath. "Once he sees her in that dumpy dress, he'll fire her for sure."

Ignoring her hurtful comment, Ellie started toward the office door.

"Stop right there!" Sputtering in outrage, the older woman stepped in front of her, pointing at Ellie in an angry staccato as she spoke. "This is the last *straw*. Whatever you might think you've earned on your *back*, you're nothing here. I've had it with your incompetence. Your *insolence!* Collect your things. You are *fired!*"

Desperately, Ellie pushed past Mrs. Alvarez into the private office of her billionaire boss.

Diogo Serrador was having a week from hell.

After a year of nonstop work and millions of dollars spent, his hostile takeover bid for Trock Nickel Ltd. had just failed.

Because he'd lost his ally on their board of directors.

Because he'd missed an important appointment.

Because his junior secretary had written down the wrong time.

And it was only Ellie Jensen's most recent mistake. For the last few weeks, he'd seen her work performance fall to ridiculous levels. He'd seen her come in late. Leave early. Take long lunches and spend far too much time hiding out in the bathroom.

Crying, probably.

Cursing under his breath, Diogo got up from his desk

and paced in front of the curved wall of windows that revealed the skyscrapers of southern Manhattan and Battery Park. For an instant, he leaned his forehead against the cool glass, staring across the New York Harbor to the distant Statue of Liberty silhouetted against the pale morning sky. In spite of Miss Jensen's inexperience, and in spite of the way he'd hired her— sight unseen, on his head lawyer's recommendation— she'd been promising enough for him to take to Rio for an important deal when Mrs. Alvarez had been ill. Ellie Jensen had been on her way to becoming a valuable asset in his office.

Too bad he'd made the mistake of seducing her.

Diogo ground his teeth. *Biskreta,* he never should have taken her to Rio. He should have fired her at Christmas, along with his treacherous ex-lawyer.

His body went tense just remembering the gleam in Timothy Wright's pale, feral face when Diogo found out what he'd done. "You should thank me, Mr. Serrador," the man had said slyly. "I saved you millions of dollars."

Thank him? The man deserved to burn in hell.

Diogo should have fired Ellie, too. Why trust a woman who was Wright's friend? But Diogo's conscience hadn't allowed him to fire her. Hadn't thought it fair.

And perhaps, he forced himself to admit, he'd liked having her in the office. Unlike many of the other secretaries, she'd always acted cheerful and kind. She hadn't stooped to gossip. She'd added brightness to his office.

Until he'd slept with her.

Diogo ground his teeth. He'd known the girl was fresh from the country, but since she was twenty-four years old, it had never occurred to him she might be a virgin. If he'd known, he never would have touched her. Virgins were off-limits. They took lovemaking far too seriously. They saw it as a *relationship*. Plus, they were usually boring in bed.

But Ellie Jensen had been so sweetly stunning. With those china-blue eyes, that angelic white-blonde hair, and the curvaceous body of a swimsuit model, he'd naturally assumed she had experience. In the heat and lust of Rio's *Carnaval*, he'd acted on impulse. Ah, and it had been such a night... His body got hard just thinking of it.

But no, he was done. There were many beautiful women in the world, and he had no interest in breaking little innocent hearts. Or encouraging naive little farm girls that they might be the ones to tame him.

He heard a scuffle outside his office door. Irritated, he turned and pressed the intercom button a second time. "Mrs. Alvarez? What is the delay?"

The door was abruptly flung open, banging loudly against the wall. He looked up, his jaw hard. "Finally. Please take a letter—"

But instead of his competent executive secretary, he saw the bane of his existence. The woman whose beauty and innocence had just cost him a billion-dollar deal.

"I need to talk to you!" she gasped, struggling with Mrs. Alvarez. "Please!"

"Miss Jensen," he bit out scathingly, then paused when he got a good look at her.

Her blond hair was pulled back in a disheveled pony-tail, and there were dark hollows beneath her eyes as if she hadn't slept. Her forehead had a pale sheen, as if she'd been ill. She looked truly awful, and her rumpled sack dress made her look as if she'd gained twenty pounds overnight. What had happened to his neat, tidy, cheerful junior secretary?

Inwardly, Diogo sighed. He should have expected this. The girl no doubt intended to tearfully confess her love for him, then beg him for a commitment.

Exactly what he'd wanted to avoid. He would have liked to keep her as his lover for far longer than a one-night stand, but he'd denied himself the pleasure. He'd purposefully ignored her, hoping that she'd realize they had no possibility of a future.

It had been difficult for him, working in the same office. Seeing her in her cubicle, he'd often wanted nothing more than to drag her back to his office and make love to her on his desk, against the wall, on his leather sofa. But he'd held himself back. He'd tried to be *noble*.

And this was the result.

Three months without a woman in his bed, and now a blown billion-dollar deal.

"I'm sorry, sir," the furious Carmen Alvarez panted, still pulling on the girl's sleeve. "I tried to stop her—"

"Leave us, Mrs. Alvarez," he said shortly.

The older woman's jaw dropped. "But, sir—"

He gave her a look that immediately caused her to back out of the room, closing the door behind her.

Diogo placed his fingertips on his wide, dark wood desk. "Sit down, Miss Jensen."

The girl didn't move. Folding her arms, she looked

up at him bitterly. "I think you should start calling me Ellie, don't you?"

Ellie? He would never be so unprofessional to refer to a member of his staff by first name. Mrs. Alvarez had been his executive secretary for ten years, but he wouldn't dream of calling her *Carmen*. But then…he'd never taken her body in the heat and madness of Rio's *Carnaval*, kissing her in the street amid the collective madness of lust…

He pushed the thought aside.

"Sit down," he repeated, and this time the girl obeyed. Her knees trembled as she sank into the leather chair across from his desk. She hugged herself, looking unhappy, almost ill. It made him feel uneasy. The look in her eyes troubled him. Made him feel guilty.

He resented the feeling. *Maldição,* he hadn't known she was a virgin! If he had, he never would have touched her!

Still. Best to have it out now. Obviously his silence hadn't given her the message. Nor had the fact that he'd taken out other women—although that had been for charity benefits and business engagements, hardly pleasure.

He would just have to be brutal. Inform her that he had no intention of ever settling down with any woman, no matter how sweet or pure or good in bed she might be.

With any luck, Ellie would accept his decision. She would return to being a competent secretary. He had to give her the chance…. Although, if a different member of his staff had made a billion-dollar mistake, he would have fired the person without thought!

But he couldn't do that to Ellie. Not after he'd seduced her in Rio on a whim. Not after he'd unthinkingly debauched the innocence of the only purely good-hearted girl he'd met in New York.

He looked down at her.

"What do you wish to discuss with me, Miss Jensen? What is so important that you nearly started a fistfight with Mrs. Alvarez?"

She swallowed. "I need…to tell you something."

"Yes?"

He waited, bracing for her to blurt out that she loved him, that she couldn't live without him, that she wanted them to move in together, or some other such nonsense. He'd heard it all before.

Instead, she said, "I… I'm leaving you." She licked her lips. "Resigning. Effective immediately."

Relief rushed through him. Then…

Sharp regret.

Regret? Ridiculous. He was just surprised, that was all. And rather sorry to lose a competent secretary.

And yet…

He sat down heavily in his chair.

"I'm sorry to hear that. But I understand why you want to leave. I'll write you a recommendation that will get you hired by any firm in the city."

"No." She shook her head. "You don't understand. I don't need your recommendation. I'm getting *married*."

He stared at her, shocked.

"Married?" The center of his chest went cold. "When?"

"This afternoon."

That soon? His hands tightened. "That's fast."

"I know."

He took a long breath. All these months, she hadn't been heartsick over him. He hadn't hurt Ellie at all by seducing her. Since then, she'd just been distracted by a hot new romance. Diogo should have been glad.

But something like cold fury went through his body. For no good reason, he had the sudden urge to punch the man who would soon have Ellie Jensen in his bed every night, doing his bidding and moaning his name. Giving him her body…

He ground his jaw. "Who is he?"

Her posture went straight in her chair. "Do you really care?"

"No." He clenched his jaw. "I don't."

She stared at him for a long moment.

"You really don't, do you?" she whispered. She shook her head. "Women are interchangeable to you. Useful only for organizing your schedule, making your coffee or warming your bed."

Warming his bed? If he'd followed his own desires, he could have had her in his bed every night for the last three months. Diogo tried to remember why he hadn't. Something about being noble. He cursed under his breath. He should have just enjoyed her. Now he'd lost the chance—forever.

He'd been replaced so easily!

Diogo had never had the experience of being left by a woman he still desired. This was his reward for doing the right thing? To see his prize carried off by some other man?

He leaned forward in repressed fury, placing his

fingers on his desk. "Useful, Miss Jensen? Hardly. Your distraction over your love affair has just caused me to lose the Trock deal—"

"I told you, call me Ellie!" she cried. "And I'm not finished!"

Feeling like a saint, he folded his arms and forced himself to wait.

She rose slowly to her feet. There was a sheen of tears in her eyes. She seemed to sway with emotion.

"I'm sorry about the Trock deal, Diogo. But there's something you need to know." She spoke so softly he could barely hear. "I'm…having a baby."

The coldness in him spread, turning to ice. A baby? Ellie was pregnant. With another man's baby.

For a second, he couldn't even breathe. He heard the echo of a woman's voice long ago, pleading in Portuguese. *"Will you marry me, Diogo? Will you?"* And later, a man's voice in the same language. *"I'm afraid she's dead, senhor. Beaten to death…"*

"Diogo?"

Ellie's voice brought him back to the present.

Pregnant. That certainly explained the weight gain and the pallor and all the time she'd been spending in the ladies' lounge. She hadn't been suffering tears of un-requited love. It had been morning sickness.

Pregnant. Ellie had been in bed with another man. Her legs had wrapped around his as she pulled him down on her naked body with an ecstatic cry of joy. How many times had they made love for her to get pregnant? Three times a week? Three times a day?

Anger rushed back in force, careening over the

numb shock like raging water filling a dry riverbed. Ever since they'd returned from Rio, he'd been celibate as a monk, striving night and day to bring the Trock deal together. And while he'd been blaming himself for taking the poor, sweet, innocent girl's virginity, she'd nonchalantly gone from his bed into a hot love affair with another man. As if her night with Diogo had been a mere stepping stone to bigger and better things.

She was pregnant.

Engaged.

And getting married in a hurry.

Suddenly, he saw the whole situation in a new light.

He sucked in his breath. He turned to face her, and his lip curved into a sneer.

"Ellie, you've got quite the act going, don't you? Playing the part of a sweet, innocent girl. But when you realized that giving me your virginity wasn't going to pay off, you quickly moved on to the next man, didn't you? You *accidentally* got pregnant. I assume he's very rich? Congratulations."

Her jaw fell open. She stared up at him in shock, her eyes large and limpid and blue as a summer storm over the Atlantic.

"You think I got pregnant on purpose?" she whispered. "That I'd force a man to marry me with a baby?"

"I think you're clever," he said coldly. "All this time I've thought you were so different from the rest—but you're just better at the game. *Biskreta,* you're the most accomplished little actress I've ever met."

"How can you even think that!"

"I'm just curious to know who the poor fool is," he said ruthlessly. "Tell me. Who's the idiot who got caught in your trap?"

He saw tears in her eyes. He steeled his heart against her fake tears, which she no doubt manufactured at will. He wouldn't let her play him for a fool. Never again! For three months, he'd worried about her feelings. He'd even denied himself her bed because he'd been trying to protect her. And all along she'd just been angling for a diamond on her finger!

Her blue eyes glittered at him through a prism of tears.

"You think only an idiot would marry me?" she choked out.

"That's right," he said coolly. "Only a fool would marry a woman who deliberately trapped him with a pregnancy."

The tears spilled over her lashes.

"Such a poised little actress," he murmured acidly. "Such a fine performance."

Looking up at him, she gave a harsh laugh, shaking her head through the tears. "*You'll* never get a woman pregnant, will you, Diogo?" she bit out. "You've made sure of it!"

"*Sim*, it is true." He bared his teeth in the semblance of a smile. "I've never met a woman I could trust longer than it takes to seduce her."

She sucked in her breath.

"And that's all you have to say to me?" she whispered. "After you seduced me and took my virginity? After three months of silence, you have nothing to say to me—but insults?"

An unwelcome shiver of emotion went through Diogo. He pushed the feeling aside. Ellie Jensen was a gold digger. It was ridiculous of him to be so surprised about it. The city was full of women who were just pretending to have a career while they tried to find a rich man.

"I do have one question," he said acerbically. "Why are you still here in my office? You've quit your job without notice. Fine. You've become such a bad secretary, I'm glad to see you go. So why are you still here? Are you afraid your marriage bed will be unsatisfying, and you're already angling to take a lover? Sorry, but I don't date married women."

She wiped her tears savagely. "You're disgusting!"

"No, *querida*. That would be you. As my employee, I respected you. But I was wrong." Wrong about so many things. First about Timothy Wright—now about Ellie. Suddenly weary, Diogo rubbed the back of his head. "Go, Ellie. Just go."

She drew back, like an ominous dark cloud rolling against the earth before the storm.

"Don't worry, Diogo," she said softly. "You'll never see me again."

Her lovely blue eyes stabbed at him with accusation. He felt troubled in a way he couldn't explain. But the moment was interrupted by a knock at the door. A security guard stood heavily in the doorway.

"Miss Alvarez called me, Mr. Serrador."

"Yes. Show Miss Jensen out," Diogo said, turning away. "Get out, Ellie. Good luck."

"Good luck," she repeated in a tight voice. "Goodbye."

He looked up, but the door had already closed behind

her. Alone in his office, he took a deep breath and leaned his head in his hands. He tried to work, but couldn't. After an hour, he gave up. He called a gorgeous actress and asked her to lunch.

It was only halfway through his martini and steak that it occurred to him that Ellie's child might be his.

CHAPTER TWO

IT WAS THE PERFECT day for a wedding.

As Ellie stepped out of the hired limousine, sweet-scented blossoms from the village's cherry trees floated through the warm spring breeze, as lush and fragrant as her pink-and-green bouquet. She could hear the sound of birds singing in the cloudless blue sky, soaring high over the white clapboard church.

It was the perfect day to start her new life as a happy wife and mother-to-be. The perfect day to forget Diogo Serrador's existence.

So why did she feel so miserable? Why had she cried for the last six hours straight, all across the Pennsylvania highway and through her hour at the hairstylist's?

"Steady," her grandmother said gruffly, taking her arm as they reached the doorway of the white church. Lilibeth's gray, bushy eyebrows quivered as she looked up at her taller granddaughter. "Are you ready?"

"Yes," Ellie muttered. But she wasn't ready at all. She'd left Timothy eight messages on the trip from Manhattan, but he hadn't answered his cell. He was likely getting in his last billable hours at his new, thriving private practice before they departed for their Aruba honeymoon.

Timothy was determined to be rich for her, he said. He didn't believe Ellie when she said she didn't need to be rich. All she wanted was to feel safe.

Safe, and to never have her heart broken again.

But she couldn't marry Timothy without telling him she was pregnant. She *couldn't*. She had to give him the option to back out of their marriage. Her hands tightened. Part of her even hoped he *would* back out…

"Careful—your flowers!" her grandmother protested.

"Sorry." With every minute that passed, Ellie's heart was pounding harder and faster. She was starting to feel dizzy. Her voice was a squeak as she said, "You promised you'd find Timothy first?"

"Are you really sure?" Lilibeth Conway squinted at her doubtfully. "It's bad luck for a man to see his bride before the ceremony."

"Please, Gran!"

Her grandmother sighed. "All right, all right. It's your day." She pushed her into a tiny antechamber inside the church, past the ushers and last few arriving guests. "Wait here."

Ellie waited. And waited. She paced, staring out the tiny window.

In the distance, she saw the rolling hills and green forests. But it wasn't all beautiful. She could see the stacks of the old, abandoned steel mill. The boarded-up storefronts. Flint, Pennsylvania, was only four hours from Manhattan by car, but felt like a world away.

She and Timothy had both grown up poor here. Returning this past Christmas as a wealthy lawyer, he'd been welcomed back to town like a hero. Timothy had already bought the nicest mansion in town and was fixing it up for her. He was spending money all over Flint, hiring carpenters and cleaners, sparing no expense. He would do anything, he'd told her, to make her love him. Anything.

But before they could marry, she had to tell him she was pregnant. Then let him decide if he still wanted to marry her.

Was it even fair to marry him like this? She took a deep breath. In spite of all his assurances that she would grow to love him, the idea of being his bride somehow felt...wrong.

But her instincts were plainly screwed up. Ellie's short-lived affair with Diogo had proven that. The night Diogo had taken her in his arms in Rio, it had felt so *right*. When he'd kissed her on the street, amid the explosion of music and bright color, she'd felt truly *alive* for the first time in her life.

Passion was dangerous. She had to try to learn to make choices with her head, not her heart.

Taking care of her mother over her long years of illness, Ellie had spent many dark nights yearning for adventure in far-off lands. For the hot kisses of scandalous men. But Diogo's hot embrace had seared her to the core. He'd arrogantly changed her whole life—and he didn't even care.

She'd wanted to tell him the truth—but how could she? Even just knowing *half* of the truth, he'd assumed the worst about her, that she was a calculating gold digger who would use an innocent baby to trap a man into marriage. He'd coldly and cruelly insulted her.

He didn't know her at all—and he never had!

"Ellie." Timothy's voice was muffled through the door, but she could still hear his affectionate exasperation. "Don't you know we've got three hundred people waiting? What do you want to talk to me about?"

"Timothy." Her whole body was still shaking from remembering what Diogo had said to her. She forced herself to take a deep breath. To steady her hands. She had to forget Diogo. She had to erase him from her mind completely and try to be glad that she would never see him again. She licked her dry lips. "Will you please come in here?"

"No—it's bad luck!"

"That's just a superstition!"

She heard him laugh. "It's taken so long to convince you to marry me, I'm not taking any chances."

Was she supposed to shout out her pregnancy confession through a door, to the shock of his ushers and the last guests walking into the church? "Please. I really, really need to talk to you!"

He paused. Then he spoke, and his voice glowed. "Whatever you have to say, I'm longing to hear it. Just wait a few minutes more, and you can tell me every day for the rest of our lives."

Horrified, she realized he thought she finally meant to tell him she loved him. Her forehead broke out into a cold sweat. This was getting worse and worse. "Timothy, you don't understand—"

"Wait," he said firmly.

She had no choice.

"I'm pregnant!"

There was a pause. Then the door flung open.

Timothy's pale, thin face was ghostly white—but he looked like he was breathing fire. He slammed the door closed behind him and grabbed her wrist.

"How is that possible," he ground out, *"when we have never slept together?"*

His eyes were so hard through his wire-rimmed glasses, his face so wild and different from his usual placid expression, that she backed up a step.

"I'm sorry," she whispered. "It was a mistake. I never meant to hurt you…"

"Who's the man?" he demanded, his slender hand tightening around her wrist.

She shook her head desperately. "It doesn't matter. I'll never see him again."

"Who is he?"

"You're hurting me!"

He tossed her arm aside. "So that's why you suddenly agreed to marry me? Because you were pregnant and your lover had deserted you?"

"No!"

"But you made a mistake if you planned to pass this baby off as mine," he sneered. "Even I'm not stupid enough to believe you're pregnant with my child, when you never let me touch you!"

"It was a mistake!" she cried. "The worst mistake of my life! I just found out I was pregnant this morning. I never intended to deceive you!"

"Right," he said sarcastically. He ran his hand through his blond, thinning hair. "Sure."

She watched him miserably. "I understand why you want to call off the wedding. It's probably for the best…"

He looked at her sharply. "What do you mean? I'm not calling anything off."

"But…"

"You're not backing out. Pregnant or not," he said in a hard voice, "you're going to marry me. Today."

She swallowed. "And the baby—"

His lip curled. "I'll take care of it."

He threw the door back with a bang and stalked out.

Take care of it?

Timothy was willing to be her baby's father?

He was truly willing to help her raise her child?

Dazed, she stumbled out of the room. She'd thought, really thought, he would call off the wedding. But he hadn't—so that meant…

She was getting married. Right now. In just moments, she would be Timothy's wife—for the rest of her life. She heard the string quartet finish Pachelbel's "Canon in D major." He'd spent a fortune on this wedding, inviting the whole town to see them wed like some kind of royal coronation. As if to force everyone who'd ever treated them badly to see them crowned king and queen of the town.

Lilibeth came toward Ellie, reaching up to kiss her cheek before pulling the gauzy veil over her face. "I couldn't help but overhear!" she said joyfully, her lips pressing an air kiss of her signature orange lipstick. "Pregnant! Oh, Ellie, I'm so happy for you, my dear!"

Happy that Ellie was marrying a man she didn't love?

Happy that the man she *had* loved was a selfish, critical, amoral bastard who didn't deserve to be any baby's father?

"But, Gran…" Ellie said softly. "I don't love Timothy."

Her grandmother's eyes widened, then narrowed. "You will," she said briskly. "You're going to have his baby."

The doors to the nave opened, and the wedding march rolled over her like a wave. People turned around in the pews, craning their heads to see her.

Standing alone at the end of the aisle, Ellie's body trembled. Her wedding bouquet shook in her hands as if an earthquake moved beneath her feet.

"Walk," her grandmother whispered with a smile, taking her arm.

Feeling numb, Ellie walked forward with Lilibeth at her side.

This felt so wrong. But how could she trust her own feelings? Her instincts had only steered her wrong. She'd fallen in love with the worst possible man in New York. Surely, she was marrying the right man now?

And she'd already treated Timothy so badly. She couldn't humiliate him further by running out of the church… Could she?

Flowers and candles were everywhere. She could feel the sharp eyes of the society matrons on her, hear the whispers of people she'd known since childhood. Old Mrs. Abernathy, who'd told her she'd never amount to anything. Candy Gleeson, the former cheerleader, who'd mocked her shabby clothes in high school and called her Stork because she'd had such a thin, ungainly body. They all now watched with envy, believing the fairy tale.

When she reached the end of the aisle, Lilibeth

handed Ellie into Timothy's keeping. He held her hand tightly, looking down at her face with a strange, almost demented look in his pale blue eyes.

"Dearly beloved, we are gathered here today…"

Compared to the broil of emotions inside her, the ceremony was so civilized. So *hollow.* The minister's beautiful words had nothing to do with how she felt inside.

She—Timothy's wife? To love him? Share his bed? Raise his children?

It had to be. Anything was better than to love someone only to be brutally rejected by them again and again. That must be how Timothy had felt, loving her for so long.

She would learn to enjoy his tepid kisses somehow. She would earn his forgiveness for her mistake, even if it took a lifetime. She *would.*

But when she closed her eyes, the memory of her night with Diogo still overwhelmed her. The way he'd ruthlessly spread her virgin lips with his own. He'd taken her innocence carelessly, like a conqueror. All the tenderness of her first kiss, the sweetness she'd timidly dreamed of sharing with a man she could love, Diogo had scornfully swept away, leaving in its place something hot and dark that burned her through, melting her to ash.

She desperately pushed the thought away. Struggling to calm the pounding of her heart, Ellie clenched her hands tighter around the green stems of her bridal bouquet. Pink and white petals fluttered slowly to the flagstones.

"Do you, Timothy Alistair Wright, take Ellie Jensen to be your lawfully wedded wife…"

Even in the midst of her wedding, she couldn't stop thinking about Diogo!

The bastard. The lying bastard.

"…for as long as you both shall live?"

Timothy looked at her. Bright light from the soaring church windows shimmered off his wire-rimmed glasses, illuminating his pale, thin face. "I do."

The minister turned to her. "And do you, Eleanor Ann Jensen, take Timothy Wright—"

The church doors opened, banging against the walls. "Stop!"

At the harsh sound of the voice, the crowd gasped. Ellie whirled around.

Diogo.

He was dressed as she'd left him in New York, in a crisply cut gray suit and blue tie that elegantly clung to his hard-muscled body. But he no longer looked anything like a civilized man of business. His footsteps echoed against the worn gray stones as he stared at her with a ruthless, demanding intensity.

"How dare you come here, Serrador?" Timothy's voice hit a high note, and he furiously cleared his throat. "You have no right—"

"You." Diogo stared at Timothy. Then he gave a hard laugh. "I should have known."

Ellie saw a depth of darkness in the Brazilian billionaire's eyes. Black, she thought with a shiver, black as a coal mine twisting deep into the earth.

"Get out of here, Serrador," Timothy spat out. "This is no business of yours."

"Is it?" Diogo turned to her with a searing intensity. "Is it my business, Ellie?"

He knew!

She took a deep, shuddering breath. She couldn't tell him he was the father of her baby. Timothy might forgive her eventually, but not if he knew that the real father was Diogo. The two men had had some kind of falling out at Christmas, and she still didn't know why.

But she did know that Diogo Serrador was as hard and unfeeling as the diamond on her finger....

He leaned forward, looking straight into her eyes.

"Is it true, Ellie?"

Biting her lip, she looked away, hiding her face beneath her veil's thick waves of netted tulle.

He ripped back her veil, and she cried out in shock. His face was so close to hers, she saw him clearly—his angular cheekbones, his rough jaw, his scarred temple, his nose that had been broken at least once.

The facade of wealthy playboy and international steel tycoon was gone. Diogo Serrador grabbed her with the brutality of a Viking barbarian claiming his woman. And a sensual current rocked Ellie's body like lightning cracking through stone.

"Tell me the truth."

She shook her head, unable to speak. She felt burned, electrified by his touch. He leaned forward, his face inches from hers, and she knew he was going to kiss her—right there in the church! While she was standing in front of the minister with another man!

And yet she couldn't lift a hand to stop him. Her knees trembled beneath her. Her bouquet dropped unheeded from her senseless fingers, falling in a splash of pink flowers against stone.

"Tell me, damn you!" His hands tightened on her

shoulders. His voice rang through the church. "Am I the father of your baby?"

Three hundred people gasped aloud. She heard her grandmother give a little choked sob. She could feel the stares of the guests. Of the shocked minister. And worst of all, she could feel Timothy goggling at her, pitiful, humiliated fury on his face.

A slow burn went through her, making her cheeks feel hot as flame.

"You have no right to humiliate me like this," she whispered. "You're the bastard, Diogo. You're the liar."

"Him?" Timothy turned on her with a look of rage. "You've kept me at arm's length for all these years—so you could give yourself to Serrador?"

"Ah." Diogo's lips curved darkly upward. His body relaxed, and his gaze glinted with sudden amusement. "So he's never even touched you. Strange way to trap a man into marriage…"

Anger raced through her. "I didn't trap anyone into anything," she spat out. "Timothy loves me. He doesn't care I'm pregnant. He said he'll take care of it!"

Diogo's eyes narrowed. In an instant, he became a totally different man.

"Take care of it?" He grabbed her arm. "What do you mean, *take care of it?*"

She felt the sizzle up and down her body. How was it possible to be so electrified by his touch—and yet so afraid? She struggled to pull her arm away.

"What difference does it make? It's not your baby. It can't be. You can't get a woman pregnant, right?" she taunted.

His dark eyes seared through her. "I am the father. Can you deny it?"

She couldn't. But she knew Diogo Serrador hadn't come to take responsibility for the child he'd created—he just couldn't bear for any other man to tread on his territory. With the arrogant machismo of a Brazilian fighter, Diogo Serrador believed he had the right to own everything and everyone. To keep them and discard them solely at his pleasure.

He didn't deserve to be a father.

"Answer me." Diogo's hand moved down her neck to the bare skin on her collarbone, to the first swell of her breasts above the white taffeta bodice. The sizzle intensified, causing her breath to come in little gasps. All the faces of guests she'd known since childhood—some watching with shocked pity, others with malicious glee—seemed to whirl around her.

Then she saw her grandmother, chalky white with orange lips. Lilibeth was the one person who'd always believed in Ellie. She'd baked her cookies on the days her mother was mean. Told her she didn't need a high school diploma to be smart. Supported Ellie during the long years she'd nursed her mother's final illness. Ellie's success had become Lilibeth's.

And now it was all ruined. Lilibeth would never be able to hold her head high in the grocery store again. *Because of her.*

"I—I—" Ellie suddenly felt faint. "I…think I'm going to…"

She couldn't even finish the sentence before her

knees started to give way beneath her. Diogo caught her up in his arms before she could fall.

"Put her down!" Timothy cried furiously.

Diogo didn't even glance his way. His dark gaze held Ellie's, reaching down into her very soul.

"The baby," he said in a low voice. "Tell me."

"No," she gasped.

He glanced at the audience gawking from the pews, then gave a single nod. *"Tá bom."*

Turning on his heel, he carried her down the aisle. He held her so close to his muscular chest that she could feel the beat of his heart.

It felt like some strange dream. The sunlight from the windows shimmered and shone around her, blurring the bright colors of ladies' dresses in the pews. Her ripped veil fluttered forlornly around her, her white taffeta train dragging behind them as he carried her out of the church, stealing her from her own wedding like a Roman centurion with a Sabine maiden.

"Come back here!" Timothy's voice was a furious squeak as he followed behind them like a yapping terrier. "She's mine, you Brazilian bastard! Do you hear me? Mine!"

Ignoring him, Diogo flung open the tall double doors.

The bright spring sun outside hit her like a slap in the face. Two of Diogo's bodyguards slammed the church doors shut behind them, trapping all the guests inside as Diogo set her gently on her feet.

But she found herself face-to-face with Timothy.

"I can't believe you did it." His wire-rimmed glasses trembled on his nose. His eyes were red and wet, fogging up the glass. "I waited for you nearly ten years. I did everything I could to win you. And you spread your legs for Serrador, who treats his women like whores?"

Every word was like a stab in her heart. "I…"

"You are mine, Ellie," he cried, reaching for her. "Mine—"

Diogo stepped between them. Carelessly, he tucked his hands into fists, widening his muscular legs into a confident stance that suggested he was ready for anything. Even in his perfectly tailored gray suit, he looked like a warrior who could fight—and kill—at will.

"Ellie's not yours. Neither is her baby. What exactly were you planning, Wright?"

Timothy's face blanched with fear. He backed away.

"Now," Diogo said softly, turning to Ellie. He brushed a tendril of hair away from her face in a gesture that was deceptively gentle. "You'll tell me the name of your baby's father."

She rubbed her forehead. "You swore on your honor you couldn't get me pregnant," she muttered. "Your *honor.*"

Diogo's dark eyes swept her face, pulling out every secret she'd ever tried to keep, leaving her vulnerable and bare. He tightened his hold on her, causing her to cry out. "I'm the father, Ellie. Say it!"

"I hate you," she whimpered.

"Say it!" he thundered.

"All right!" she shouted. Tears of grief and rage streamed down her face. "You're the father!"

Timothy gave a loud, high moan. She turned to him desperately. "I'm so sorry. So sorry…"

She tried to reach for him, but he slapped her hand away. Bitterly, he turned to Diogo.

"Take her, and be damned. She's filled with your child. It disgusts me. Another whore for you. Another bastard—"

Diogo punched him hard across the jaw. Ellie screamed as Timothy dropped like a stone into the lush green grass.

The Brazilian turned to her, and the rage in his eyes made her draw back in confused fear. He blinked, staring at her. His dark eyes suddenly looked sad, as if haunted by shadows and ghosts of long ago.

Then he abruptly turned away without a word. At his signal, two black sedans pulled forward on the street. As a bodyguard opened the door, Diogo pushed her gently into the backseat, holding her against the leather as he drew the seat belt over her body. She struggled, but his grip was implacable. His hands were like iron shackles wrapped in silk.

And every accidental brush of his fingertips made her feel fire in her veins. How could she fight her own desire? How? She swallowed, trying to control the pounding of her heart as she glanced through the back window.

"Timothy—"

"He'll have a headache." His teeth gleamed in a feral growl. "He deserves worse."

Why? What had Timothy done? But she didn't have the nerve to ask. She had far more pressing issues to worry about. "Where are you taking me?"

"To the airport." He sat next to her as the driver pulled away. She could feel his thigh pressing against hers through the layers of her wedding dress.

He looked down at her, his eyes black as onyx. Then he gave her the heavy-lidded half smile that had led so many women to ruin.

"Now," he said, "you belong to me."

CHAPTER THREE

By the time the private plane touched down in Rio de Janeiro, Ellie knew without doubt that Diogo was a soulless barbarian without a drop of mercy.

They'd left from a small private airport tucked in the rolling hills of central Pennsylvania. He'd carried her onto an enormous private plane waiting in a hangar. Ignoring her questions and demands, he'd locked her into a small ensuite bedroom in the back of the plane. She'd been alone since the plane took off. For sixteen hours, she'd had nothing to do but cry and sleep and eat snacks from the small refrigerator. And wonder what he meant to do with her.

Now, you belong to me.

What did that mean?

She shivered, holding her ripped wedding veil tightly in her hands.

Diogo had made it clear he had no intention of getting married. Shown that he did not like or even respect her. And his playboy lifestyle was hardly conducive to being a father.

So why had he kidnapped Ellie? Where had he taken her?

She placed her hands on her belly through the wrinkled taffeta of her wedding dress. In just one day, she'd already come to love this baby more than her own life. To vow that she would treat the little boy or girl—for some reason, she thought it might be a girl—very differently than her own mother had treated her. Ellie would treat her child with love. *Ellie would protect her.*

She clenched her hands into fists. Diogo might think he could still boss her around, but she was no longer his employee. He would soon realize how much had changed between them...

She heard the bedroom door unlock. Diogo entered the small cabin of the plane, newly shaved and wearing fresh clothes. In his crisp white shirt and tailored black pants, he appeared relaxed and self-confident. He'd no doubt had an excellent night's sleep. Unlike her.

"Welcome to Rio de Janeiro," he said with a smile, holding out his hand. "I trust you slept well?"

She rose from the bed, folding her arms with a scowl. "Rio? No! Take me back!"

"Back to your precious bridegroom?" Coolly, he withdrew his hand. "No. You will remain with me until the baby is born. I thought I made that clear."

Kept prisoner by the most ruthless playboy in the world, in a strange, exotic city? A whimper escaped her lips. She wanted to go home. She wanted her grandmother. She wanted to be a million miles away from this man who'd so carelessly seduced her, lied to her, and lured her into heartbreak.

She raised her chin. "You can't keep me here against my will. I'm going home the first chance I get!"

"This is your home now." He gave her a lazy smile. "But Rio can be dangerous. You must stay close to me. For your own protection."

But who was going to protect her from *him?*

She looked wildly at the door behind him. "I'm not going to stay with you!"

"You have no money or friends here. You don't even speak Portuguese. I'm curious. Exactly how do you intend to escape?"

"Somehow," she whispered, but uncertainty raced through her. Everything he'd said was true. How on earth would she get home?

"Forget Wright," he told her coldly. "He cannot help you. Obey me, and it will be easier for everyone. Especially you."

Obey him?

That was what had gotten her into this trouble in the first place. In the alley off Copacabana Beach, amid the rhythmic beat of samba music and cries of the crowds, he'd taken her in his arms and kissed her with a sudden ferocity that had made her weak. "You're coming home with me now," he'd whispered against the flushed heat of her skin. "You can't say no."

And she'd been desperately in love with him then as only an innocent girl could be. All she'd wanted was to be utterly his. To give herself completely. And she'd naively believed that he would give himself to her in return, body and soul.

She no longer believed in those frosted, sugar-coated dreams. She knew better now. She knew to play it safe.

Diogo Serrador was a million miles from safe.

She shook her head desperately. "You said you would never want to marry any woman because of pregnancy. Fine. Send me back home. We'll never bother you again. The baby will never know you're her father!"

Diogo's dark eyebrows lowered. "Because you and Wright have other plans for him?"

She thought of Timothy's angry words, the hurt in his eyes. But he'd always been good to her. He'd even offered to take care of her baby. Marrying him would have been such a sensible, respectable choice, but now she'd ruined everything. She suddenly felt like crying. "He's a good man, and I promised to be his wife."

"Forget it," he said with a curl on his lip. "You're not leaving Rio."

He marched her out of the plane.

The rush of jungle humidity and the smell of exotic flowers hit her like a blow in the deep violet darkness of dawn. Clouds were pouring a brutal onslaught of rain, pounding heavily against the leaves, leaving puddles on the tarmac of the small private airport.

A bodyguard held an umbrella over their heads as they descended the steps from the plane. Ellie balanced precariously on her four-inch, white satin heels, her wedding gown dragging through the water as Diogo steered her into the backseat of a waiting steel-gray Bentley.

Giving a calm order in Portuguese to the chauffeur, he leaned back against the supple leather seat.

"Don't do this," she said tearfully. "Please. Let me go back."

"To Wright?" His eyes were dark. "You still love him after he called you a whore?"

Pain wracked through her. She briefly closed her eyes, taking a shuddering breath.

"You wouldn't understand," she whispered. How could he understand her guilt and shame? She was desperate for Timothy's forgiveness after she'd treated him so badly. "We have known each other since I was fifteen years old—"

He cut her off. "You will never see him again." He reached his arm around her in the backseat of the Bentley, pulling her close to his body. "Now you belong to me."

For one brief instant, she relished the warmth and weight of his strength. Then she caught herself. Horrified at his power over her, she forced herself to pull away.

"You only want me because you think you can't have me."

He looked down at her. "Is that what you think?" he asked huskily. "You think I can't have you?"

"It's what I know." Her heart was pounding in her throat. "You are a liar. A thief. A heartless playboy. I'll die before I let you touch me again."

"Touch you how?" He stroked down her neck, tracing the bare skin of her collarbone. It was like an electric shock down her body. "Touch you like this?"

"Don't." One brief touch of his hand against her skin, and she trembled all over. "Please."

"Please what?" He stroked her cheek to her tender

bottom lip, causing heat to race from her lips down to her pregnancy-swollen breasts. Her nipples tightened in a sudden shock of desire as he gently ran his hand down the valley between them.

"Please," she whimpered. She closed her eyes, barely able to breathe. "Please stop."

"That's not really what you want." She felt his hand move over the smooth taffeta of her bodice, cupping her full—and very sensitive—breasts. Her nipples sizzled with painful sensation.

Gently, he pulled down the fabric. He lowered his head to taste her bare breast. She felt his lips move against her aching nipple, suckling her, swirling her taut flesh with his tongue.

Her whole body reacted. She gave an involuntary gasp as her back arched into his mouth.

He was right. *She did want this.* All her hatred and pain of the past few months had done nothing to end her longing for his touch…

Oh my God, what was she thinking? The chauffeur was driving the Bentley, pretending that he couldn't hear or see anything. Probably because this was normal for Diogo to seduce women in the backseat of the car. Ellie was just another in a long line of his lovers. He would seduce her just to prove his power, make her love him again, then discard her and the baby like rubbish. Diogo Serrador was a selfish, hard-hearted playboy to the core.

Had she lost her mind? She couldn't give in to him. Not like this.

Not ever.

"No," she whispered. With a huge effort of will-power, she shoved him away. "I said *no!*"

Sucking in his breath, he looked down at her. His dark eyes were deep with need…and something more. Some hidden emotion—some secret pain that lured her to believe she could be the one to comfort and save him…

She—comfort and save Diogo? She fought the ridiculous thought with all her might. He didn't need saving. He was a selfish, lying, coldhearted bastard!

Diogo abruptly released her, leaning back against his seat. "You will soon accept your fate," he said coldly. "Until my son is born, you will submit to my will."

She feared he was right—but what could she do?

Exhausted, Ellie leaned her head against the window. Her long, blond hair had long since fallen out of the sleek wedding chignon. It was a total mess, along with her taffeta wedding gown. As the Bentley traveled the back streets of Rio, following his bodyguards' sedan, she shivered as she looked out at the violet-gray dawn of the passing city.

"What do you intend to do to me?" she whispered.

He opened the *Jornal do Brasil* to the business page. "I will keep you until my son is born."

"To keep me?" Her voice trembled. "As your prisoner?"

Lowering the newspaper, he looked at her coolly. "Whatever it takes."

She swallowed. "And the baby?"

He gave her a grim, humorless smile. "Do not worry."

"How can I not worry?" She exhaled in a rush, and turned to stare out blindly at the heavy rain sheeting the car window. "I'm her mother."

"Was that really your plan?" His voice was mocking, but when she turned her head, his eyes searched hers. "Did you intend to be a mother?"

Was he still accusing her of being a gold digger and deliberately getting pregnant? "Of course I never *intended* to get pregnant," she said angrily. "You are the one who—"

"In my experience," he interrupted, "a woman who fancies herself *in love* will give up anything to keep her lover."

Humiliation made her cheeks hot. Did he realize how she'd foolishly loved him?

"Anything," he added quietly. "Even a child."

Did he want to take her child from her?

"No!" she gasped. "I would never give up my baby!"

He looked down at her. "We'll see if that's true." He looked away, out the window. "Once we're home."

She swallowed in sudden fear. His penthouse at the Carlton Palace was a fortress. He owned the top two floors, one for his personal use and the floor beneath for his bodyguards. Once he installed her there, he could keep her imprisoned. He could take her baby. He could do anything he wanted.

He could truly make her his possession.

It was where he'd taken her virginity. Where he'd made her cry out with joy. Where they'd created their baby by making love all night. On his bed. Against the wall. He'd tasted her, shoved into her, wrapped her legs around him and made her cry out again and again until she thought she'd die of pleasure…

I cannot get you pregnant, querida.

"You are such a liar," she whispered.

He glanced at her swiftly, his eyebrows lowering. "I never lied to you."

"You said you couldn't get me pregnant. The truth is that you were just too selfish to use a condom!"

Abruptly he folded the newspaper, setting it down on the leather seat between them. "I didn't lie."

She choked out a laugh. "But I'm pregnant!"

"I'd had a vasectomy in January. I put off the follow-up appointment. I just assumed it had worked." He clenched his jaw. "I later discovered my mistake. Now, it is truly complete."

She looked at him. "Complete?"

"It is now absolutely impossible for me to get any woman pregnant."

"That's very comforting," she said bitterly. "Thanks for clearing that up. But since you're so determined never to be a father, why did you take me from my own wedding?" Her voice trembled. "Let me go, and you'll never have to see the baby. You can forget the pregnancy even happened and go back to your actresses and swimsuit models."

"Sorry." He looked at her. "I can't do that."

"Why?"

"Because he's my son." Reaching out, he stroked her cheek. "And as long as you're pregnant, you're my woman."

His woman?

"What do you mean?" she whispered. "Do you intend to marry me?"

"Marry you? No." He bared his teeth in a smile. "I'm

not the marrying kind. Even if I were, I certainly wouldn't marry a woman who's in love with another man."

She stared at him, her jaw agape. "I'm not in love with Timothy!"

"No. You're just desperate to be with him." He looked scornfully at Timothy's nine-carat, yellow diamond engagement ring on her finger. "So much that you were willing to marry him with my child in your belly. Without telling him. Without telling *me*. And you don't love him?"

She flushed. "I had no choice—"

"You don't have a choice now." He leaned forward, his face inches from her own as he gently tucked a tendril of hair behind her ear. "You will forget him…"

At Diogo's touch, a rush of heat went through her, firing up the longing in her blood. She had to resist the urge to press her cheek against his hand. Her lips tingled, aching for his kiss.

No! She wouldn't fall for his seduction again!

She had to get away before he could hurt her again. Before he could hurt their baby. Because a man like Diogo could only be trusted to make you love him—and then leave….

Her pulse hammered as she clenched her fists tightly. "You don't care about me or this baby!"

Drawing away from her, he bared his teeth in a smile. "I do care…about my son. I will keep him safe."

She blinked at him. "Safe from what?"

He looked down at her grimly. "Safe from you."

Safe—from her? As if she would hurt her own child?

Bewildered fury went through her. Diogo was the one who'd caused this whole situation—he'd gotten her pregnant then kidnapped her against her will, and yet he dared to say that *she* was the dangerous one?

Oh, she had to get back home. She needed Lilibeth. She needed her grandmother to take her into her arms and tell her everything was going to be all right.

Outside the car window, the pale pink sun broke at last through the clouds, illuminating the dark warren of houses crammed onto the hillside. Rio's favelas were famous. But from this angle they didn't look so bad. Sprawling out over the hillsides, they looked more like San Francisco's exclusive, luxurious neighborhoods than poverty-stricken slums.

Rio can be dangerous, Diogo had warned.

But he'd just been trying to scare her. And Ellie was no longer scared.

She was *fed up*.

Diogo had broken her heart. Humiliated her at her own wedding. Hurt people she cared about. Taken her against her will to a country where his power was absolute.

She wasn't going to wait around until he seduced her, turned on the charm and lured her into loving him again. Because she knew the instant she and the baby started to count on him, he would grow tired of playing house. He would abandon them and merrily go back to his life as the playboy of New York, amusing himself with every beautiful woman who caught his eye.

He'd had a vasectomy to make sure that he would never have a child. Why should Ellie risk her child's heart and security with a man like that?

The Bentley pulled into a side street that was nearly deserted in the early-morning downpour. It stopped at a traffic light. As Diogo leaned forward to speak with the chauffeur, Ellie saw the bodyguards' sedan pull far ahead of them.

It was her only chance!

She wasn't going to be any man's prisoner…

Flinging open the car door, Ellie ran into the rain, her wedding dress illuminated white as she fled into the dark sanctuary of the slums.

CHAPTER FOUR

THE DARKNESS WAS SINISTER, lit with only bits of light from glassless windows covered by ragged fabric. Alleys curved like grasping fingers over the hillside, stretching across the slums in broken half streets of cracked concrete slick with rain.

Ellie had barely turned down the first alley before she knew she'd made a horrible mistake. She tripped on the uneven ground, tumbling into a tumult of taffeta skirts. She felt a sudden pain in her left wrist and an involuntary sob escaped her lips.

"Onde você está indo?"

A man came out of the shadows. Behind him, a younger man with blackened teeth jeered, looking her up and down. *"Você está perdida, gringa?"*

She didn't understand their words, but the insolent way their eyes stripped her naked screamed danger. Using her unhurt hand, she pushed herself up.

"Excuse me," she whimpered, backing away. "I'll go…"

The younger man blocked her path, even as a third man appeared from the shadows. All three surrounded her, coming closer until she could see their leers in the semidarkness.

"What a pretty bride," the first one said in heavily accented English. "I'll have that big diamond off your finger, *gringa*."

Her hands trembled as she pulled off Timothy's engagement ring and threw it on the ground. She hoped it would distract them long enough for her to get away. She turned to run, but the younger man stopped in front of her. He gave her a smile, and she was close enough to see his missing teeth and smell his foul breath.

"Now," the first man said in thick English behind her, "I'll have that dress…"

She screamed as the men closed in.

Suddenly, Diogo was between them, protecting her. He fought off the first man with a punch then a round kick, knocking them all back. The ferocity in his eyes, gleaming in the sharp burst of light as lightning crashed across the narrow bit of sky, scared her—even as she clung to him in the danger of the favela.

The older man pushed past the others, narrowing his eyes as he looked at Diogo with recognition. "Serrador," he sneered, then spat on the ground. *"Você está aqui em férias?"*

"Sai fora, Carneiro," Diogo said. His lip twisted as he added in English, "This woman is mine."

The other man gave a harsh laugh as he motioned his companions forward. "You were stupid to come back here."

Diogo moved swiftly, whirling against the three men,

keeping Ellie carefully behind him. In a series of supple, acrobatic movements, he pushed his attackers back with one sweeping kick after another. He dropped into a one-handed cartwheel, kicking his opposite leg upward in a fluid, deadly blow that snapped back Carneiro's head. Diogo slammed into the second man with an elbow punch, and knocked the third to the ground with a crack of his skull against the man's forehead. Cursing him, the men stumbled away into the darkness.

Ellie turned with a pounding heart to watch them disappear into the shadows from whence they'd come. Then Diogo grabbed her shoulder, whirling her around.

"You little fool," he ground out. "They'll be back with more. I should just leave you here!"

"Do it then!" she cried. "I'd rather take my chances with them instead of you!"

His hand tightened on her shoulder, spreading shock waves through her body. She forgot the pain of her wrist. Something started trembling deep inside her.

"You're eager to give your body to ten or twelve men?" he said furiously. "To be passed from one man to the next?"

She blanched at his crude suggestion. Then clenched her hands into fists. She wouldn't let him succeed in scaring her. "I want to go home!"

"Back to your lover?" he sneered.

"Timothy's not my lover!"

"But you are desperate to return to him—desperate enough to risk our child's life!"

"I would never risk our child!" she gasped.

"You ran away!" Lightning flashed again and she

saw the dark fury in his eyes. "Do you know what would have happened if I hadn't found you in time?"

Aftershocks of terror washed over her. Diogo was right. She'd risked her baby's life!

"And all because you are so *in love,*" he said scornfully.

"I'm not in love with him! I was only going to marry him because I couldn't have *you!*" she cried out, then covered her face with her hands. "I just want—to—go ho-ome!"

Another flash of lightning crashed above them. She barely felt the rain pounding against her wet clothes and skin, barely heard the warm wind howling in her ears.

Then suddenly he took her into his arms.

"Shh, Ellie," he whispered, tenderly kissing her temple. "It's all right. Everything is going to be all right."

He held her close, caressing her tenderly. But his kindness only made her cry harder.

Diogo was right to be angry, she realized. What if he hadn't found her in time? What if he hadn't been able to save Ellie and their baby from her foolish decision to run into the slums? What would have happened to them—*because of her?*

"I can't believe I did it," she whispered. "I put our baby at risk!"

"It's my fault," he murmured against her skin. "I was wrong to scare you. You're safe now, *querida.* Both of you."

He scooped her into his arms as if she weighed nothing at all. Both of them were wet with rain in the desolate gray alley of Rio's slums, and yet somehow, cradled against his chest, Ellie suddenly felt warm...and safe.

Maybe it really was going to be all right, she thought in a daze, looking up at his handsome face. Maybe she'd been wrong. Maybe she could trust him after all…

"Come, *querida*." His expressive, dark eyes shone down at her. "Let me take you home."

CHAPTER FIVE

ELLIE'S EYES FLUTTERED OPEN. She saw bright morning sunlight sparkling on the waves of the ocean. Outside the car window, food vendors were opening colorful umbrellas on the white sand of Copacabana Beach. People were already gathering on the beach to work and play, wearing the tiniest of bikinis or even club clothes from the night before. Cariocas let nothing stop their pursuit of pleasure…*just like Diogo*.

Diogo!

She sat up straight, realizing to her horror that she'd fallen asleep on his shoulder. Not only that, but she'd even drooled a bit on his shirt!

"How—how long was I sleeping?" she whispered.

He smiled down at her. "About twenty minutes."

"Oh." Her cheeks went hot. She surreptitiously gave her mouth a wipe. What was wrong with her? She'd never fallen asleep around Timothy. Not once. Of course, he was a stable, steady, respectable guy. Her screwed-up instincts could apparently only relax cuddled up in the backseat of a Bentley with the dark playboy of the Western world!

I'm just tired, she told herself. Since she'd gotten pregnant, being tired was a constant state of existence. But why did the safe man make her tense—and the dangerous one make her feel so relaxed? There was something really, really wrong with her.

The Bentley pulled beneath the porte cochere of the Carlton Palace. Ellie looked up at the 1920s white-stucco landmark, a luxury hotel and condominium resort in elegant Louis-XV architecture like a wedding cake.

"Do you remember this place?"

Of course she remembered. She'd seen it constantly in her dreams: the place where he'd seduced her. The place where he'd made her drop every shred of decency she'd ever known, along with her clothes…

She shivered as heat flashed through her body, causing a bead of sweat to form between her breasts. "Yes."

Once he took her upstairs, there would be no escape. He could do whatever he wanted to her. Anything. If he wanted to seduce her, she wouldn't be able to resist. He could just reach out and take her. She wouldn't be able to stop him.

If she *wanted* to stop him…

Getting out of the car, Diogo came around the Bentley to open her door himself.

"You said you were taking me home." She looked up timidly. "This isn't my home."

"I want it to be." He held out his hand. "But you are wet and tired. We can discuss all that later. For now, you need rest, food, a hot shower." When she didn't move, he said, "Please. Give me the chance to treat you with the care you deserve."

A shower and breakfast sounded like heaven. But even more captivating was the smile he gave her as he held out his hand. That smile won her over as all the force in the world couldn't.

She looked down at his strong, muscular hand. He had thick, masculine forearms, laced with dark hair. The hand of a fighter. He'd already proven that. But it was also a hand that could make her lose her mind with his sensual, masterful caress....

"All right," she said with a deep breath. "I'll give you a chance."

His larger hand enfolded hers as he helped her out of the car. She trembled at the touch of the fingers that had once touched her in such unspeakable ways. The last time they'd been in Rio, he'd done such things to her virgin body that even now, her breath constricted just remembering.

You're so beautiful, he'd said hoarsely, *I will die if I don't have you.* She remembered the swirling pleasure of his tongue, so bewildering and like nothing she'd ever imagined. The sensation as he slowly thrust one finger inside her...then two...then three. The mastery of his kiss. The way he'd teased, demanded, enticed her. His sensual onslaught had made her tremble and explode. She'd whimpered and thrashed and bucked against his mouth. He'd held her down firmly with the weight of his muscled body, so masculine and foreign and strange and... *Oh my God, my God, Diogo, I love you, I love you, I do.*

She could hardly believe that three months ago, she'd let him strip her naked and seduce her into ecstasy she'd never known existed. And when he'd realized she was a virgin and tried to pull back, she wouldn't let him release her. Trembling at her own boldness, she'd held him tight. She'd never wanted to let him go.

So much had happened since then. He'd gotten her pregnant. Lied to her. Ignored her.

But something had changed in the favela. What? What had made him suddenly relax back into the charming man she remembered? He'd suddenly started acting almost as if he truly cared about her....

No! She couldn't start thinking that way. Who knew where such dangerous thoughts would end?

He led her inside the hotel, past soaring ceilings, palm trees, gilded furniture and the elegant check-in desk. But Ellie barely noticed. She had eyes only for Diogo. In a small, private elevator, he turned a key to push the button for the top floor. The doors slid open and he led her past two bodyguards lounging in the hallway. They nodded at him respectfully, barely bothering to glance at Ellie.

But why should they notice her? They probably saw him with a different woman every night. She was just the latest in his long line of lovers. Tomorrow, he'd be with somebody else.

The thought chilled her like a shadow.

"You're shivering," Diogo said, observing her keenly as he unlocked the door to the penthouse.

Her teeth chattered. "No. I'm fine, really."

"Come inside. I will soon get you warm."

Following him in a daze, she kicked off her muddy high heels and stepped on the thick white carpet inside.

It felt good to take off the painful shoes, but nothing else in this penthouse was particularly comforting to her. The decor was severe and Spartan—modern, minimalist and cold. Glass and metal sculpture was placed sparingly against the white walls. High floor-to-ceiling windows edged the penthouse, surrounding a freestanding, two-story-high white fireplace.

It was the most sophisticated home she'd ever seen. Elegant, certainly, and very expensive, but severe and about as friendly and warm as an ice pick.

As Diogo closed the door behind her, she idly rubbed her bruised wrist. It was still sore, but no longer had the same sharp pain.

"You are hurt?" he demanded.

"It's nothing. I fell on my wrist earlier—"

"Let me see," he ordered.

She reluctantly held out her hand, protesting, "It's much better now. Really. You don't need to…"

Then he touched her, and she sucked in her breath. Fire spread up and down her body as he examined her, gently moving her hand to the right and left.

"Your wrist isn't broken," he said, releasing her. "I spent ten years learning capoeira on the streets. I can recognize a break or sprain. You have neither. But if it hurts, I will call the doctor and she can…"

"No, really," she breathed. "I'm fine." She couldn't stop looking at his handsome face. At the sharp lines of his jaw, his high cheekbones, the slightly crooked nose that gave him the hard look of a warrior. His sensual mouth. The lips that she longed to feel against her skin…

He looked up at her, and his dark eyes seared her.

"What do you want first?"

First? She licked her lips. She wanted him to make love to her with heat and urgency. To whisper hoarsely against her skin that he wanted her and only her forever. To say he wanted to be a good, loving father to their baby, and that he would always, always…

"Ellie?"

"What?" Nervously, she tucked her hair behind her ear. "What do I…?"

"Breakfast first? Or—no." Cursing himself under his breath, he shook his head in sudden decision. "I'm being stupid. Of course, we should start by taking off your clothes."

It was as if he'd read her mind. "My…clothes?"

What was she thinking? No, no, no! She couldn't allow this to happen!

Clutching the wet wedding dress against her body, she backed away. Every step she took left a wet trail against his floor. "I won't be your mistress, Diogo," she said aloud, willing herself to believe it. "I won't be your latest one-night stand!"

"Why do you think that's what I want?" he asked quietly.

Her heart turned over in her chest. He wanted more? She licked her dry lips. "What else could it be?"

"You're pregnant with my child. I want you…to be comfortable and warm. You're soaking wet, *querida,* chilled to the bone. You need a hot shower. Breakfast. Dry clothes."

Of course. Ellie wanted to kick herself. Of course that was what he'd meant. Did she actually think he was desperate to seduce her? Now there was a laugh! Diogo could have any perfect woman he wanted—and not just the vapid beauties, but smart, gorgeous women who ran their own businesses and had college degrees. Not high school dropouts like Ellie! Her cheeks went hot with humiliation.

He came toward her, reaching for her dress.

"No." She stumbled back from him, suddenly unwilling to let him touch her. "I don't need your help."

He snorted. "That wedding dress weighs more than you do. Come here."

With calm arrogance, he reached for her.

Like a coward, she turned and ran blindly into the next room. She saw a round wall of windows overlooking Copacabana Beach and the Avenida Atlântica far below. In the center of the room was a bed, large, white and stark.

His bedroom. She bit a knuckle in consternation. The last place she wanted to be! Whirling around, she tried to escape but he was standing in the door. She started to shut the door in his face, but he easily blocked her.

"Obrigado, querida," he said with a sensual smile. "This will be much easier."

He came forward and pulled her tightly against his body, then unzipped the back of her gown. Ellie's damp skin felt suddenly cold against the air. Her body felt light, freed of the heavy weight of her dress as he pulled the thick, wet skirts down to her thighs with a single hard yank. She watched yards of taffeta fall to her feet.

And she realized she was standing in front of him with nothing but a white silk bra and panties that clung transparently to her skin.

With a gasp, she tried to cover her breasts with one arm and panties with the other. He gave her a smug, masculine smile.

"I can see you naked anytime I want, Ellie," he said, sounding amused. "All I have to do is close my eyes."

He was laughing at her modesty! A flash of anger went through her.

"You have so many women in your bed," she snapped, "I'm sure it's someone else you're picturing. I'm not a bit worried!"

"I see," he murmured silkily. "Surely you're not jealous, *querida?*"

"Of course not," she huffed. Of course she was. She tossed her long, wet hair. "You can sleep with every supermodel in Brazil for all I care! It's not like I have any reason to…"

Her strident voice faltered as Diogo turned away from her, pulling off his wet white shirt and dropping it to the floor. Distracted by the vision of Diogo's hard chest, impossibly covered with muscles and scars of a warrior, she couldn't finish her sentence. His tanned skin was etched with black hair that descended from his broad shoulders down his flat belly. His rain-dampened gray trousers clung to his hips and fit buttocks as he went into the adjacent bathroom.

She heard him turn on the shower. Heat flooded her cheeks—and everywhere else in her body. What was wrong with her? How could she still want him so badly when he'd made it clear that, aside from her pregnancy, he didn't find anything about her particularly interesting or special?

Folding her bare arms, she shivered in the wet silk bra and panties clinging to her skin. Three months ago, Diogo Serrador had taken everything from her. Her innocence, her faith, her courage in her dreams. Was she really such a desperate fool that she was willing to throw herself under the same train again, the Serrador Express that stopped for no woman?

And worse, it was no longer just her own heart and soul at risk. Now she had her child to think about. When Diogo left, as he inevitably would, he wouldn't just abandon Ellie. He would leave behind a heartbroken child who would always wonder why her father hadn't loved her enough to stay.

Just like Ellie's father. He certainly hadn't loved them enough. He'd been forced into marriage by a baby—Ellie. He'd married her mother, he'd been Ellie's father. Sort of. He'd mostly spent years on the couch after work, watching mindless television and drinking beer, barking at Ellie or her mother if they ever dared to ask him a question.

Then when her mother had gotten sick, just when they needed him most, he'd packed up his bag. "Sorry," he'd muttered to fifteen-year-old Ellie without meeting her eyes. "I've just got to take my own happiness while I can."

And so Ellie had dropped out of school to take care of her mother, working nights at the Dairy Burger to support them. Her mother had accepted her care bitterly, blaming Ellie as the cause of her miserable marriage and all her own missed chances.

Ellie's child wasn't going to grow up that way.

"Ellie," Diogo said. She looked up and saw echoes

of her own pain in the dark depths of his gaze. It was so tempting to reach out to him. To try to protect him from whatever had caused that hidden anguish in his eyes.

But what was she thinking? Diogo need her help? That was a laugh!

"You're shivering."

She turned away. "I'm just cold."

He reached out to stroke her cheek.

"So let me warm you," he whispered.

Pulling off her bra and panties, he lifted her naked body up into his arms. She was too numb to protest as he carried her into the marble-and-steel bathroom. He carried her into a tall, freestanding shower surrounded by a round wall of clear glass and pushed her gently inside.

She gasped as hot water hit her skin. It caressed her body, running down her hair, her throat, between her breasts. Down her belly to the tuft of hair between her legs. So hot, so sensual, so *alive*. For so long, she'd felt nothing but heartache. She'd felt so numb when she agreed to marry Timothy. What difference did marrying him make? She almost hadn't cared if she lived or died.

Until she found out she was pregnant…

She heard Diogo enter the shower behind her.

With a sudden intake of breath, she closed her eyes, realizing he had to be naked. Awareness surged through her body as she leaned her hot forehead against the glass. She knew his hard, muscular body was just inches from her own, his muscles caressed beneath the same streaming hot water. She moved as far away as she dared, pressing her body against the glass.

"Please don't touch me," she whispered, not turning around.

"You want me to touch you, *meu amor.*" His accented voice was deep, barely audible above the sound of rushing water. He put his hands on her shoulders, slowly rubbing the knots of tension with his thumbs. "And I want to touch you. I've wanted it for months. It has nearly killed me not to touch you."

He hadn't forgotten her? He'd missed her?

But even as she told herself it couldn't possibly be true, she leaned back against him. His hands felt so *good.* Stress and anger and fear melted away beneath his ministrations.

He slowly rubbed her shoulders.

Then her back.

Then…

Her whole body felt pink and warm and limp as he turned her around in his arms. She closed her eyes, as if she could pretend she weren't naked in front of him. As if every inch of her skin weren't crying out for his caress, to feel his body hot and hard against her own.

She felt his arm around her naked waist. His muscular thigh pressed between her legs. "Open your eyes, *querida.*"

She shook her head.

"Ellie."

"No."

He ran his hand down her naked back, against her soft skin that was already slick with wet heat. Involuntarily, she shuddered beneath the stroke. She pressed her hands back against the glass, struggling to steady the sway of her knees.

"What do you want from me?" she whispered. "After all these months of ignoring me?"

"I stayed away to protect you." He took a deep breath. "You were a virgin. I feared you would take our affair too seriously, that you would want things from me I could not possibly give."

"Like—like a commitment?"

His voice was low. "Yes."

Unthinkingly, Ellie's eyes flew open. "I know you'd never commit to any woman—"

Her voice trailed off as she looked at him.

The glass of the round shower was opaque with steam, leaving them in their own white world, utterly alone and far too close. Broad-shouldered, he towered over her, every inch of him hard with muscle. His masculine brutality frightened her. Her eyes glanced between his heavily-muscled legs and she sucked in her breath.

He scared her. And yet…

She wanted him. So badly.

She licked her lips. "And now?" she managed hoarsely. "What has changed?"

"You are pregnant with my child. There is no question of me letting you go." Leaning close, he stroked her wet hair back from her face. "Until the baby is born, you are mine…."

He ran his hands down her hot skin. Down her arms. Down the valley between her breasts to her belly. She felt his fingers slowly run along her hips, lightly brushing her waist and pausing to caress the new fullness of her belly.

He lowered his lips to hers.

His embrace was as hot and demanding as it had been during *Carnaval*. He kissed her deeply, roughly, biting her lips until they bruised. Then his embrace became more gentle. His arms wrapped around her body, holding her close. He took her swelling breasts into his hands, cupping their weight, squeezing her sensitive nipples between his fingers.

A soft cry escaped her lips as he bent his head beneath the hot water. He teased one nipple with his tongue as he crushed the other in his hand. The whole world seemed to swirl around her, around and around with the sweet agonizing pressure of the water—and his tongue.

With a little cry, she arched her back.

"I am the only man who's ever touched you like this," he whispered in her ear. She felt the dark scruff of his chin against the tender skin of her neck. "Tell me."

"Just you." She sighed.

"Ellie." She felt his fingers, soft as a whisper, brush against the hair between her legs. A hard shiver rocked through her body as she gasped for breath. She threw her head back against the glass, trembling to her toes. The warmth and closeness of the shower crowded in upon her, the hot waves of pounding water rushing down the curves of her body.

He was so close. So close. And she wanted him closer still. Wanted him to pick her up in his arms, press her against the glass and thrust inside her until she forgot her own name. Until she forgot every pain and regret. Until she soared with the explosive joy she hadn't felt since the day he'd left her....

He stroked between her legs with deliberate, agonizing slowness.

"Please," she whimpered, twisting her head from side to side against the glass. "Please!"

"Please what?" he said softly. He lowered to kiss her, biting her neck.

She could feel him leave a mark on her skin. As he'd long ago left a mark on her soul. He'd already marked her in the deepest way possible: he'd filled her with his child.

"Tell me what you want, Ellie," he murmured against her skin. "I want to hear you say it."

What did she want?

A cry rose up from her heart. A man she could love. A man she could trust with both her child and her heart.

She wanted the impossible.

Tears rushed into her eyes.

"Isn't it bad enough that my baby will be born without a name?" she whispered. "Bad enough that I'm an unwed mother—bad enough that everyone thinks I'm your whore? Are you so selfish that you want to make it true? To take the last bit of pride I've got left?"

He froze. Looking down at her in the shower, his expression was half-shadowed in the light of the translucent bathroom windows.

She had the vision of his muscular body in the sunlight flickering through the hot steam, standing proud and fierce like an ancient god of fire. An all-powerful heartless Greek god who seduced mortal maidens at will and left them cold and starving for his fire until the day they died.

He looked away.

"I never wanted to hurt you, Ellie," he said in a low voice. "Never."

Abruptly, he turned off the hot water.

Without another word, he pulled her from the shower. He dried her off with a thick cotton towel, then did the same to his own muscular body.

And even as she trembled beneath his touch, she still couldn't look away from his perfect masculine form, the dark hair on his chest and belly forming a perfect arrow down to his...

She squeezed her eyes shut.

She told herself she didn't want him. And even if she did, *she couldn't have him*. The pleasure he offered was like a drug. One more taste, she would never escape the addiction.

Diogo was a selfish womanizer. He took what he desired. He grabbed a woman and didn't let go until he'd had his fill; then he tossed her aside for the next one. He cared only for his own pleasure.

She heard him leave the room and waited to hear the front door slam. Now that she'd denied him his instant gratification, he would move on to some other, more compliant woman.

She closed her eyes. He would easily find another woman to satiate his desires. A woman a thousand times prettier and smarter than Ellie would ever be.

"Ellie," he said.

Shocked he'd returned, she opened her eyes. He was dressed in a black shirt and dark jeans. He held out something for her.

Taking the pile of clothes in her arms, she saw a

lovely dress, panties, a bra in her size—all stretchy enough for her expanding shape, but soft and very, very pretty. The kind of maternity clothes that cost a small fortune.

"Where—how did you—"

"I had my staff arrange a wardrobe for your stay."

"My—stay?"

He gave her a slow-rising smile that she felt down to her toes. "Come with me."

CHAPTER SIX

ALL THROUGH BREAKFAST, Ellie couldn't stop giving Diogo little furtive glances over the table.

Sitting on the sunny warmth of the penthouse balcony, with a wide vista of the Atlantic Ocean and the sharp, cragged peak of Sugar Loaf Mountain rising to the east, she watched Diogo drink black coffee. Watched him smile and chat easily in Portuguese with the housekeeper. Watched him eat his buttery croissant slathered in jam with obvious pleasure.

So different from Timothy, who ate his meals with surgical disinterest. Diogo enjoyed his life. Even the little moments.

Sitting with him in the Brazilian sunshine, breathing sea air that was fresh from last night's rain, Ellie realized that she was enjoying herself, as well. She wiggled her toes in her comfortable new sandals, then sat forward in her chair and accepted the housekeeper's offer of a second ham-and-cheese omelet.

For some reason, for the first time in forever, Ellie felt…hungry.

Happy.

She sipped sparkling water from a crystal stem. Finishing her ham-and-cheese omelet, she gobbled down two chocolate croissants, all the while gulping down papaya, mangoes and *açai* berries, washing it down with sweet-tart *pitanga* juice. Every bite was ecstasy. Every taste better than the last. She felt good down to her bones.

And every time she looked up from her plate…

She saw him.

Their eyes met, and a shiver went through her. He hadn't left her when she refused to make love to him. He hadn't run out to look for some other woman. He hadn't even been angry. He'd just brought her outside to share a meal with him in the sunshine.

Almost as if he cared.

She bit her lip, trying not to even think such things. She couldn't start to imagine he cared. She couldn't count on someone who would inevitably fail and abandon both her and the baby. It was better that her child have no father at all!

Growing up with a distant father and bitter mother, Ellie had promised herself that her life would be different. She would fall in love with a man who loved her desperately in return. They would marry and have a family. Children. Grandchildren. Through all their lives, they'd have a love affair that never ended.

But real life wasn't like that, was it?

At least—she thought with sudden sadness—it wasn't like that for her. But she'd be a fool not to enjoy this moment while she could. Breakfast with Diogo in

Rio. A beautiful, sunny morning. Delicious pastry and comfortable shoes…

Reaching forward, she helped herself to another chocolate croissant. She sighed as she took a bite, enjoying the exquisite flavor. She'd try to follow Diogo's example. If she couldn't have her impossible dreams, she would try to savor the pleasures of the moment while she could!

The housekeeper refilled Diogo's coffee, and he nodded her dismissal. When he was alone with Ellie on the balcony, he leaned across the table.

"Pregnancy suits you."

Mouth full, she looked up to discover Diogo looking at her with frank desire. An electric current traveled between them.

"You're even more beautiful," he said, "than you were that day at *Carnaval*."

Feeling awkward, she swallowed the bite of fruit and leaned back in her chair. Forgetting her gracefully placed linen napkin in her lap in her confusion, she wiped her mouth with her sleeve.

"Thank you," she muttered.

"How are you feeling?"

"Great." And to her amazement, it was true. The nausea she'd felt for months was gone. In fact, she hadn't really felt sick since she'd arrived back in Rio and taken a deep breath of the fragrant air, spiced with exotic flowers and the salt of the sea.

"Good." Diogo smiled at her. "I have a proposition for you."

A little thrill zinged through her. "A proposition?"

A fantasy overwhelmed her brain. *I want you, Ellie, you and only you. I want to raise our child together. I want to marry you and make love to you every day for the rest of our lives...*

Stop it! she yelled at herself. Hadn't she learned not to dream impossible dreams—and learned it the hard way? Besides, she didn't want to be Diogo's wife. Why would she want to marry a man she couldn't even trust to be faithful?

"Ellie." He took a sip of his coffee, then set down the cup. "You are so young."

She snorted. "Twenty-four!"

His dark gaze seared her. "That is young to me. You are barely starting your life. You had no intention of getting pregnant, but I caused you to conceive my child. You shouldn't suffer because of my mistake."

She gave him an uncertain smile. "I haven't exactly been suffering..."

He gave her a brief, humorless smile. "I've caused you to be sick for months. Driven you out of your job. Kidnapped you from your wedding... Shall I go on?"

"What is your point?"

"I caused this," he said quietly. "I can fix it."

She clasped her hands beneath the table to hide their trembling. "How can you fix something like this?"

"I want you to promise to stay with me."

Her heart leapt up into her throat. "To promise?"

"Until the baby is born. Then you can go back to New York, or anywhere you desire. You can return to your career, if you like. You can date whomever you want. Being pregnant has thrown you—it's what nearly made you marry a man you did not love. It clouded your judgment. Marrying him would have ruined your life—and my son's."

"What are you driving at?" she whispered.

"After our child is born, I will set you free." He took another sip of coffee. "My son will stay with me."

A dagger of ice passed through her body. "You want to separate me from my baby?"

"It is for the best, Ellie. You never wanted to be a mother—"

"That's not true!"

"And I'm not convinced that you can take proper care of him."

Her jaw dropped. "You can't be serious."

"I am."

She sucked in her breath.

"You think you would be a better father?" she demanded furiously. "You'd never even be home! You fling yourself into a new woman's bed every night!"

"Ellie, listen—"

"No, you listen to me!" She abruptly rose from the table. "You're the one who doesn't have the ability to be a good parent. The baby and I are leaving right now—"

"Stop," he ordered, and she stopped. She heard him come behind her. He placed his hands on her shoulders. The weight of them pressed down on her like the burden of her heart's hopeless yearning.

He turned her around in his arms.

"You will stay here until the child is born," he said. "That is nonnegotiable. I can't take the chance you might return to Timothy Wright—or any other man like him. You will remain here where I can keep an eye on you."

She fought back tears. The Brazilian sunlight must have glazed her *brain* to make her think that she could ever trust Diogo! "So you can keep me prisoner, you mean!"

"So I can keep you safe," he said coldly. "You don't know Wright as well as you think you do."

"I know he's my friend. I know he's got more honor and decency in his little finger than you've got in your whole body!"

He gave her a grim smile. "And it's that blind lack of judgment that shows you're not fit to raise my son. I simply cannot trust you to—"

"You can't trust *me?*" she gasped. "That's the most ridiculous thing I've ever heard! You are nothing but a rich, spoiled womanizer who's never had to struggle for anything in your life. While all I want, all I've *ever* wanted, is to take care of the people I love!"

He ground his jaw. "I do not want a custody battle, Ellie. Give the baby up to my care. He will be happy and secure." He paused. "And I will compensate you for your trouble. I will make you rich beyond your wildest dreams."

"What?" she gasped, confused. What did money have to do with custody of their baby?

"Ten million dollars." He looked down at her. "I will give you ten million dollars to go."

For a moment, she couldn't breathe.

Then outraged fury rushed through her. "No!"

"Is ten million not enough?" He leaned closer to her, his black eyes holding an unfathomable darkness in their depths. "You're holding out for twenty?"

"I won't sell her for any price!"

"Him," he corrected unthinkingly. "You have a price. We both know you do. Just tell me what it is."

"I don't want your money, I just want you to let us go!"

"A hundred million dollars. That's my final offer, Ellie. I advise you to take it."

A hundred million dollars.

She stared at him in shock. It was an unimaginable number. And Diogo meant it. She could see it in his eyes. A powerful billionaire like Diogo Serrador could make a single call, and the forty dollars in her bank account would instantly be transformed into a hundred million dollars.

He truly thought he could buy her baby. Just like that.

His reckless arrogance made her catch her breath. What kind of man would think he could buy and sell anything he wanted—even the precious relationship between mother and child?

"But you don't even want to be a father!" she choked out. "You had a vasectomy. You don't want children. Why try to take mine?"

He clenched his jaw. "I had the vasectomy to make sure that no child of mine was in the world without my knowledge, to be hurt by someone who doesn't have the judgment or resources to be a decent parent."

Fury raced through her.

"And you think you'd make a decent parent just because you're rich? You've never been able to commit to anyone for longer than a week. You'd likely grow bored raising a child and abandon her. I wouldn't choose you as my child's father if you begged me!"

The hard look in his eyes could have shattered diamonds into dust.

"Agree to my terms, Ellie. Until the baby is born, I'll treat you like a queen. Then you will be a rich woman, free to pursue life and enjoy your own romances to your heart's desire. What is your answer?"

She clenched her hands. He really thought she would sell her child to the highest bidder then go gallivanting off to find a boyfriend and spend her millions?

She set her jaw, facing him with eyes full of hate.

"My answer? That's easy," she spat out, clenching her hands. "*Go to hell.*"

Go to hell?

Diogo cursed softly in Portuguese.

He was already *there*.

He'd been a fool to sleep with Ellie in the first place. An employee—a small-town girl—a virgin. What had he been thinking?

He hadn't been thinking. That was the problem. Returning from an all-night deal in Rio, triumphant over an acquisition, they'd been stopped on their way back to the hotel when their car was halted by an impromptu street celebration along the Avenida Atlântica. Samba music and dancers had poured from Copacabana, some samba dancers dressed in sequins and feathers, others barely dressed at all.

Diogo had pulled Ellie from the car. He'd cleared a path for them, walking the last blocks to the Carlton Palace. They'd passed an alley where a man was making love to a woman against a wall. As he kissed her lips and caressed her breasts, a different man knelt reverently between her naked legs.

Diogo was a Carioca by birth. He hadn't been shocked. But he'd instinctively glanced back at his wholesome junior secretary trailing behind him, her hand clinging tightly to his own. He'd seen her look in the alley, and her pink lips had parted in a hoarse intake of breath.

And then she'd turned and looked straight into Diogo's eyes.

Wordlessly asking him to touch her.

Begging him to taste her.

Suddenly, amid the frenzied celebration of the music-filled *batucadas* swaying to the frenetic rhythm filling the air like exotic perfume, he'd really seen Ellie Jensen. Not just as a beautiful girl, but a pure-hearted beauty, skin white as snow, hair like spun gold. Ellie had been so desirable that it had made him hurt inside. As if he'd gone back in time to when he'd still believed in love and fidelity…

He shook his head. Love? *Abestado*. He'd stopped believing in that particular fairy tale long ago. But he'd known then that he had to have Ellie or die.

People lost their minds during *Carnaval*. They discarded marriage vows without repercussion or blame. Diogo had briefly lost his senses beneath the pounding rhythm—nothing more and nothing less.

He didn't remember how he got her upstairs to his penthouse. He just remembered the way she'd trembled beneath him in bed. Her gasp of pain and his own shock when he'd discovered she was an untouched virgin—not wholesome just in appearance, but reality. He'd tried to pull back, but she'd reached up and kissed him with lips so tender and sweet that all possibility of stopping was swept away. He'd thrust into her slowly, inch by agonizing inch, until he heard another slow-rising cry rise from deep inside her. He made her come again, and then a third time, until the tears in her eyes were from pleasure too great to bear.

Only then did he finally allow himself to surrender. He thrust inside her, imploding with an explosion of white heat that made him collapse against her on the bed.

Afterwards, he'd held her. He made love to her all night. And far more surprising—he'd slept in her arms. He still remembered the feel of her soft, gentle body. Knowing that when dawn came, he would have to give her up.

Biskreta, he grew hard just thinking about that night.

Staring at her now, even as he demanded that she leave both him and the baby forever, he wanted her back in his bed. Craved her beyond all reason. Beyond all resistance.

But he couldn't trust her. Ellie was young, naive, shortsighted. If Diogo hadn't guessed the truth about his baby's paternity, he would never have even known that he existed. Ellie would have married that bastard Wright. *She would have given his child away.*

Did she know what kind of man Timothy Wright was? Did she have any idea how he'd suddenly gotten so rich over the last few years—his nasty little side business?

Diogo intended to find out.

"A hundred million dollars is a lot of money, Ellie. It's far more than Wright would have gotten for you."

Her china-blue eyes widened. "What are you talking about?"

He watched her narrowly. "Don't you know?"

She shook her head, and her lips turned down in a sad little moue. "I just know I treated Timothy badly," she whispered. "He's loved me for ages. But I couldn't love him no matter how hard I tried. Then I humiliated him in front of all our wedding guests…"

Diogo barked a laugh. "He deserves far worse." Suddenly haunted by the image of a woman's face, he looked away. "I nearly killed him at Christmas. With my bare hands."

"Why?" He heard Ellie take a step toward him, heard her intake of breath. "What did he do?"

"Do you really want to know?" he asked harshly.

She put her hand on his arm. "Yes. I want to know."

He looked up at her. Ellie had changed a great deal from the shy secretary he remembered. Her body had changed, as well. He could now see the unmistakable signs of pregnancy. Her pale skin glowed. Her slender breasts had grown huge. They swelled beneath the pretty neckline of her maternity dress, straining beneath the fabric.

He found himself picturing what those new breasts now looked like. What they felt like.

How they tasted.

Maldição, she was the most alluring woman he'd ever met. And she didn't even realize her own power…

His whole body broke into a hot sweat. Desire went through him with an unbearable force that made his hands tremble. He wanted to toss her onto the bed, take her hard against the wall, to thrust into her again and again until he satiated this agonizing need…

He clenched his hands, turned away. He had to get a hold of himself. It wasn't like him to be so close to losing control!

"Ellie," he said in a low voice, "do you know how Wright was getting so rich?"

"Timothy's private practice in Flint was thriving—"

"He's been buying and selling babies on the open market," he ruthlessly interrupted. "Taking children from poor mothers and giving them to rich, childless couples who can afford his illegal fees."

She stared at him, her mouth agape. Then she shook her head violently. "No! Timothy wouldn't do that!"

"Before your wedding, you told him you were pregnant with another man's child. What did he do?"

All the color slowly drained from her face.

"He told me he'd take care of it," she whispered. "But I thought he meant… I thought…"

She sucked in her breath. Then covered her face with her hands. "Oh my God."

Diogo stared at her.

Ellie hadn't known.

She hadn't intended to sell their child.

Not for love.

Not for money.

She'd just turned down Diogo's offer of a hundred million dollars. How many women would have done that? None of the greedy debutantes or avaricious actresses of his acquaintance. They all would have made noises about loving their child and wanting to be a good mother—but for a hundred million dollars, they would have tripped over themselves trying to shove the baby in his arms.

He had his proof. Ellie Jensen was…not a gold digger.

She was just foolish and blind. She'd given her precious virginity to Diogo, knowing that he had no intention of being a husband or father. Then she'd agreed to marry an unscrupulous, rotten man like Wright, because she actually thought he would be a good father for her child.

Like most women, Ellie was weak. But she wasn't immoral. She wanted to protect this baby, just as he did. She placed the security and happiness of her child above her own desires.

And that changed everything.

"I'm sorry, Ellie," he said quietly. "I had to know what kind of woman you really were. I had to know that you wouldn't hurt our child."

She wiped the tears from her face. "And now that you know?"

Now that he knew? Diogo still wanted to protect his child.

But he also wanted Ellie in his bed. To have her every night and make love to her until he was utterly satiated. He took her in his arms.

"I want you to stay with me, Ellie. Raise our child together. I want you to remain in my bed for as long as the sweetness lasts."

She took a long breath. "And then?"

He stroked her cheek, forcing her to raise her chin. "We will always be parents, Ellie. Even when we cease to be lovers."

Looking up into his eyes, the expression on her face changed.

"Damn you," she whispered. "I won't be your toy."

"Yes," he said with absolute certainty, "you will."

And he kissed her.

CHAPTER SEVEN

HIS KISS WAS TENDER and pure, but Ellie felt the hunger beneath his embrace. Diogo's demand matched her own, threatening to consume her and burn her in his fire.

He wrapped his arms around her. He towered over her, so much taller and stronger than she, and Ellie felt captive in his arms, unable to pull away. But it was her own longing that trapped her, holding her as no act of force possibly could. His body was hard and warm against hers. The fresh wind blew from the ocean, twisting her blond hair around them, and she felt the hot Brazilian sunshine against her skin. The world seemed suspended in time as his lips demanded the surrender she longed to give.

She realized she was holding him as tightly as he held her. Her fingers clutched his back as his tongue teased hers, causing a sigh to rise from deep in her throat.

She knew she should stop but she wanted another minute in his arms. Her whole body begged for *just one more minute...*

But no matter how she wanted it, she couldn't let this happen.

To Ellie, making love to a man meant *being* in love,

while to Diogo it was nothing but a moment's pleasure, swiftly forgotten before the next break of dawn.

Diogo's hot kisses lured her to her own destruction.

"Ellie," he whispered against her hair. "Come to my bed. Now."

Her heart pounded. She pressed her cheek against his chest, barely able to breathe for the pounding of her heart. "It wouldn't be wise."

"Why?"

She licked her lips. "I told you...I can't just be your one-night stand."

He ran his hands through her blond tendrils, down her bare arms. "You're far more than a one-night stand to me."

She looked up at him. "I am?"

"We will always be connected, Ellie." His dark eyes crinkled as he smiled down at her. His charming, arrogant, impossible-to-resist smile. "You are the mother of my child."

Only that.

In spite of herself, her heart sank in her chest. She should have been glad. That Diogo would wish her to be his mistress, and that he'd be an active partner in their child's upbringing, was far more than she'd once dared hope.

But it no longer satisfied her. Her stupid, greedy heart wanted more. She wanted to be able to make love to him and be secure in his arms. To know that she could trust him with her heart. To know he would forget about pursuing other women, all those beautiful women with brilliant careers and college degrees....

He gently raised her chin. "I will always respect you, Ellie. Always honor you."

"But no one else will," she whispered. "Everyone will assume just what you did—that I'm a gold digger who purposefully got pregnant. They'll always treat me like your whore."

A rough Portuguese curse escaped his lips. "I will kill any man who dares call you so."

She shook her head as tears rose to her eyes. "It doesn't matter. The real question is, can I trust you to be a good father?"

He drew himself up, affronted. "What?"

"You've never committed to any woman for longer than a week. Can I truly trust you to love a child for a lifetime?"

"Those two things are entirely different!"

"No." She shook her head fiercely. "It's the same. It's love. It's loyalty—"

"I will never abandon a child. Do you understand me, Ellie? Because I know what it feels like. I had no father. When I was eight, my mother abandoned me to leave the country with her newest lover." He looked away, clenching his jaw. "I would never do that to my child."

She stared at him in shock.

"But you're a Serrador," she said, bewildered. "Your father owned half the gold mines in the world before he died. Your older sisters married European royalty. You were rich by birth, long before you made your first million in the steel business!"

His cruel lips curved. "That's the story."

"Isn't it true?"

He grabbed her arms, looking down at her. "What is true is that I want you, Ellie. Raising my child. And in my arms. In my bed." He stroked down her cheek to her neck and rubbed her plump breast with his thumb, making her nipple ripe and taut. He whispered, "And I always get what I want."

He lowered his mouth to hers in a searing kiss. She felt the hardness of his body pressed against her. She wanted nothing more than to surrender.

She couldn't resist Diogo's desire. His strength. His power. His heat.

As he kissed her, Ellie's fingers curled around his crisp black shirt. She felt his lips like a current through her body, felt the wind in her hair as they stood in the sunshine on his penthouse balcony over Copacabana Beach, and she could no more push him away than she could stop breathing.

She had to give in. *She had no choice…*

Blood rushed loudly through her ears. Then she realized the buzzing was the sound of his cell phone vibrating from his pocket.

With a muffled curse, he glanced down at the phone to see the number. His expression changed.

And then he pulled away from Ellie to answer the call!

"Bom dia," he said warmly. "Catia. *Eu vou mais tarde? Por favor!"*

Ellie blinked at him in shock, struggling to regain her senses. She listened to the tender, almost pleading sound of his voice, and her cheeks went hot with humiliation.

Two minutes ago, he'd been kissing Ellie, intent on seducing her into his bed.

But he'd already forgotten all about her. He'd ditched her mid-kiss in his eagerness to talk to another woman!

I must be out of my mind, she thought, putting her hands on her head in consternation. *Truly insane!*

Diogo put his hand over the phone. "Excuse me," he said as coolly as if Ellie were still just his employee. "I will return in a moment."

She watched him leave the balcony through the sliding glass doors. Shocked and fighting back tears, Ellie whirled back around to stare blindly toward the vista of Copacabana Beach and the wide blue sea.

She'd been so close to giving in!

How could she have thought she could possibly trust Diogo? He was nothing like the calm, steady, loyal man she needed. Nothing like Timothy…

But wait. Timothy wasn't a good man, either.

He's been buying and selling babies on the open market. Taking children from poor mothers and giving them to rich, childless couples who can afford his illegal fees.

Timothy a cold, calculating baby seller? She still found it hard to believe. Although it was true she had been uncomfortable around him at times. When he'd first proposed, she'd been only fifteen, working long hours at the Dairy Burger and struggling to take care of her sick mother. Timothy had been twenty-five, a fresh graduate of Yale Law. She'd been incredulous at his first proposal, but he'd kept trying. He'd even offered to support Ellie and her dying mother.

But she hadn't wanted Timothy's charity. It wouldn't have been right to take advantage of his feelings, or make him think their relationship could ever be more than friendship.

Until last year. With her mother gone, Ellie'd had no reason to remain in Flint…and Timothy had offered her something she couldn't resist. A job in New York City.

Perhaps she'd been wrong to accept. But she couldn't kid herself that she would have gotten her job without his help. All of Diogo's other secretaries had not only finished high school, they'd graduated from college. And yet, against all odds, she'd done well in her position of junior secretary. She'd learned quickly. She'd been popular with the other employees.

At least until Jessica had spread the rumors far and wide that Ellie was trying to climb the corporate ladder by climbing her boss.

She sucked in her breath. Maybe she really was the slut they all thought she was! She'd nearly agreed to be Diogo's mistress, knowing that he'd never marry her. Knowing that he would never even *love* her, and when he tired of her in bed he'd move on. Knowing that all the world would believe her to be a gold digger—a greedy secretary who'd retired from her job as soon as she'd gotten pregnant by the boss!

Diogo came back onto the balcony. *"Com licença, querida,"* he murmured, reaching for her. "Now. Where were we?"

She jerked away with a gasp. "You must be kidding!"

"You are upset?"

"Because you were kissing me, then stopped to take a call from another woman!"

His eyes grew cold. "You do not own me, *querida*.

Do not presume to think you have the right to know my secrets."

"Why shouldn't I?" she demanded, fighting back furious tears. "From the moment you first seduced me, you've acted like you own me. Like I'm your possession to ignore or enjoy as you please—"

There was a cough as one of the bodyguards slid open the glass door to the balcony.

Diogo turned on him with a scowl. *"Sim?"*

"A médica está aqui, senhor."

Diogo's eyes were still dark as a midnight storm as he turned back to her. Clenching his jaw, he said, "The doctor is here."

"Doctor?" she repeated, still scowling.

"Yes."

"But I told you. My wrist is fine!"

"The doctor's not for your wrist. She's for our baby."

Our baby. Hearing those words on his lips did strange things to her insides—made her want to forgive him anything. She desperately fought the feeling!

"Since you only just realized you were pregnant," he continued, "I'm guessing you didn't have much prenatal care in New York?"

She shook her head. "Just a drugstore pregnancy test."

"I thought as much. From now on, my son will have the best quality care. Letícia is coming to give you a checkup, an ultrasound."

Letícia? He called the doctor by her first name?

Diogo suddenly smiled, and his handsome face glowed with charm. "Come. Enough arguing. Let us see our baby."

He held out his hand, waiting.

See their baby. There was no way she could resist something like that…

Ellie reluctantly placed her hand in his. As she felt his fingers enfold her own, a sizzle went through her—not just desire, but of something more.

Completeness.

No! She could allow herself to imagine they were a family. A real family loved each other, protected each other—trusted each other. Diogo and Ellie might raise a child together, but they could never be more than two single parents….

She told herself these things, but her body wouldn't listen. As he led her inside from the balcony, she couldn't stop the feeling of rightness.

This man is for you, her body insisted. *You are for him.*

As Diogo smiled down at her, her heart give a strange new flutter—a sensation different from any she'd ever felt before. She marveled at the masculine beauty of his face. The bright Brazilian sunshine caressed his olive skin, haloing his black hair, making him handsome and dangerous as a shining dark angel.

"*Você está pronta, meu amor?*" He lowered his head to kiss the knuckles of her hand. "Come, my love. Let's see our baby."

CHAPTER EIGHT

AS THE DOCTOR FINISHED Ellie's preliminary checkup, Diogo left the study to take a phone call.

A phone call that involved business...or pleasure?

Don't think about it. Ellie clenched her fists as she stared up at the ceiling. She knew Diogo wouldn't answer questions, anyway.

She glanced at the dark-haired, thirtysomething Dr. Carneiro, who was now preparing the equipment for the ultrasound.

Another of Diogo's mistresses?

Dr. Carneiro spread a clear gel over the gentle swell of her naked belly, and Ellie murmured, "It's very nice of you to make a house call like this."

"I'm happy to do it," she replied in accented English. "Anything for Diogo."

She called him *Diogo?* Ellie bit her lip.

"You are a lucky woman, Miss Jensen," the woman continued.

The fear in Ellie became intolerable. "And you know this how?"

The slender, dark-haired woman glanced at her. "Ah.

You think I was his lover?" She gave a merry laugh. "I am his *sister*—or the closest he's ever had."

Relief flooded through Ellie. "But I thought your last name was Carneiro."

"It is. I'm no Serrador!" the doctor replied indignantly. "Those half sisters of his don't deserve to shine his shoes. No. My mother brought him home to live with us when he was eight. She found him shivering on the streets."

"Your mother saved him?" Ellie blurted out. "After his own mother abandoned him?"

The doctor nodded grimly. "But he's saved all of us since then. He paid for my college. He hired my younger brother Pedro as his most trusted bodyguard. He would even have helped Mateus, if he'd been willing to leave the favela." She sighed. "But my older brother is too proud. He refuses Diogo's help."

Carneiro. The same name as the leader of the men who'd attacked Ellie in the favela. "I...think I might have met him."

Dr. Carneiro looked sad. "Diogo will win him over eventually. It took him years to win Pedro's loyalty, but Diogo never gives up. He funds my free clinic which helps thousands of people every year, people in desperate need of care. New mothers. The elderly. Sick children who would die without the medicine he provides." She looked at Ellie. "You are fortunate. Not all men are so honorable— or so strong. And after what happened at Christmas—"

"Talking about me, Letícia?"

Diogo stood in the doorway, looking none too pleased.

"You know I can't stop praising you." Dr. Carneiro

FREE BOOKS OFFER

To get you started, we'll send you
2 FREE books and a FREE gift

There's no catch, everything is **FREE**

Accepting your 2 **FREE** books and **FREE** mystery gift places you under no obligation to buy anything.

Be part of the Mills & Boon® Book Club™ and receive your favourite Series books up to 2 months before they are in the shops and delivered straight to your door. Plus, enjoy a wide range of **EXCLUSIVE** benefits!

- Best new women's fiction – delivered right to your door with FREE P&P
- Avoid disappointment – get your books up to 2 months before they are in the shops
- No contract – no obligation to buy

We hope that after receiving your free books you'll want to remain a member. But the choice is yours. So why not give us a go? You'll be glad you did!

Visit **millsandboon.co.uk** to stay up to date with offers and to sign-up for our newsletter

2 **FREE** books and a **FREE** gift

P9CI

Mrs/Miss/Ms/Mr   Initials

BLOCK CAPITALS PLEASE

Surname

Address

Postcode

Email

MILLS & BOON®
Pure reading pleasure

gave her adopted brother a warm smile. "And you're just in time. Look."

Moving the wand against the goop on Ellie's belly, she pointed at the monitor. Ellie looked, as well, and instantly forgot everything as she saw the tiny flicker of her baby's heartbeat on the monitor.

Diogo's hand suddenly reached for hers. He sank into a nearby chair, his eyes similarly riveted on the monitor. "That little light….that's our baby?"

"That's the heartbeat," Letícia said. "And there, you can see the legs…the spine. The head. Do you see?"

"A boy?" he asked.

"It's early to be absolutely sure, but do you see that? Yes. A boy, I think."

"A boy!" Diogo exulted.

"And there, you see…" She suddenly frowned. "Wait. That's not… It can't…"

The doctor's voice trailed off as she stared at the monitor with her brow furrowed. Ellie felt Diogo's hand tighten around her own.

"What is it? What's wrong?"

Ellie glanced at him. His handsome features were anxious and vulnerable as he looked from the monitor to the doctor. Ellie realized he was trying to hide his fear.

And the thought struck through her like lightning: *he loved this child as much as she did.*

"What is it?" Heart in her throat, Ellie could barely manage to whisper the words. "What's wrong with our baby?"

Dr. Carneiro turned to face them, her thin face lit up with a smile.

"You're going to have a girl."

"A girl!" Ellie crowed happily. She turned to Diogo triumphantly. "Ha! You see? I told you it would be a girl!"

"Not a boy?" Diogo said, frowning.

"Yes," the doctor said.

"What?"

"A boy…and a girl. The girl was hiding behind her brother."

Ellie and Diogo both blinked at her, uncomprehending.

The doctor gave a laugh. "Look." They stared where she was pointing. In all the unrecognizable lines and blurs of the monitor, Ellie at first couldn't see what she was talking about. Then she saw it. Another tiny flickering light. Other arms and legs. Another shape of a head. Another baby.

"Two heartbeats. Twins. Congratulations!"

"Twins?" Ellie gasped.

Two babies to love. Two babies to care for. Two babies who would need everything their parents could give them!

Sucking in her breath, she glanced at Diogo. Just a few months ago, he'd had a vasectomy to prevent having a child. Now he was going to be father of two. A readymade family. How would he take the news?

"Have you picked any names?" the doctor asked.

Ellie shook her head. "It's all happened so suddenly. We haven't really thought about it." She tried to see Diogo's face. "We could call the girl Lilibeth. Or maybe Lily?"

He finally turned to face her. Ellie was shocked to see his dark eyes were bright with unshed tears in his handsome, rugged face. "She will be called Ana."

"Oh, that's wonderful!" his sister exclaimed. "Our mother would be so proud."

Ellie lifted her chin and pleaded, "But my grand-mother…"

"My daughter's name is *Ana,*" he informed her coldly.

Ellie ground her teeth. Just like a man to not listen to anyone's feelings but his own! But on the other hand, if his adoptive mother really had saved him from starving on the streets, it seemed a small enough thing to ask.

She closed her eyes. "Ana," she tried aloud. "Ana Jensen." Opening her eyes, she nodded. "All right. Ana."

But Diogo didn't look grateful. He stared at her, his dark brows lowered.

"Jensen?" he demanded. "Their last name will be Serrador."

She shook her head. "You expect me to raise the babies in Flint with a name different from mine?" she protested.

"Raise them in Flint?" he thundered. "Are you out of your mind? You are going to live here with me— all of you!"

"I might stay until they're born. But longer than that? You can't honestly expect me to remain here forever, se-questered in your penthouse like some trapped princess in a tower!"

"I *thought,*" he ground out, "that we could raise the children together. I am their father."

She nodded. "And you will always have access to the children. We'll work out custody. But—" she raised her chin "—you are not my husband. You will not have access to *me.*"

* * *

Twins.

Looking back at the heartbeats on the monitor, Diogo suddenly saw everything clearly for the first time.

He'd thought that it was enough for him to bring Ellie to Rio. To take care of her, to keep them all safe. But now he saw that he'd been wrong…so wrong.

A son. A daughter.

Without his name.

His precious newborn children wouldn't be protected. They would be…*bastards*. Just like Diogo had been.

He still remembered the pain of his childhood. First he'd had no father—then later, no mother. No money. No home.

He'd had to toughen up fast.

He didn't want his children to grow up that way. He had to protect them. He had to keep them safe.

His hands gripped the edge of the sofa as he looked up again at the blinking lights on the monitor.

He heard the plaintive whisper of a woman's voice from long ago. *Will you marry me? Will you?*

But he hadn't asked her questions; he'd just been furious. Marry her? He'd been incredulous that she would try to pin him down after three dates in as many weeks. *If you don't care about me,* she'd whispered, *then I'm done with you.*

He'd never seen her again. He'd forgotten her swiftly. Until he got the call from the Brazilian lawyer at Christmas last year. *She was just found—beaten to death. Your name was in her will.*

Diogo's whole body was tense as he clenched his

jaw. He wasn't going to make that mistake again. Too much was at stake. Ellie was his new chance to do it right—from the very start. The happiness of his children depended on it.

Allow Ellie to take them to the States?

What kind of home would it be for them, caught between two continents, between two families? His children would barely know their father. Perhaps they, too, would hate him....

Maldição, he swore soundlessly, no! He would not let his children suffer—not let them be torn away from the father that loved them! They would be respected. They would be loved.

By *both* parents.

Ellie was traditional, not like the modern women of the age who were happy to make a go of parenthood alone.

Isn't it bad enough that my baby will be born without a name? she'd cried. *Bad enough that I'm an unwed mother—bad enough that everyone thinks I'm your whore? Are you so selfish that you want to make it true? To take the last bit of pride I've got left?*

He could solve this problem. For all of them.

Suddenly, it was all so clear.

He looked straight into Ellie's eyes.

"You will marry me."

Ellie's jaw dropped. "What?"

He'd never thought he would propose to any woman, but it was strangely easy. "You will stay here. We will raise our children together. It is simple, Ellie. You will be my wife."

He waited for her to exclaim with joy, to throw her

arms around him, to proclaim her thrilled gratitude. But she didn't.

She *flinched*.

"Stop it, Diogo. We know you're not the marrying kind."

He frowned at her. "I've changed my mind."

"Just stop it!" Blinking hard, she turned to the doctor. "The babies are healthy, aren't they? My cycle has never been even, so I didn't even take a pregnancy test until recently. But I never drank alcohol or—"

"Do not worry. They look fine," the doctor said soothingly, glancing between them. "The pregnancy is going well. You'll just need to take good care of yourself." She gave Diogo a hard stare. "You'll need to help her."

"*Sim,* of course." *Biskreta,* he was trying to take care of her as he'd never taken care of any woman—he was trying to make her his bride! Leaning forward, he persisted, "Ellie, I am serious. I wish to marry you."

She cast her blue gaze on him, then looked away. She didn't believe him.

The thought was ironic. He'd never thought he would so willingly give up his freedom, but here he was, begging a woman to marry him. Only to have her turn him down!

But Ellie would be his. Diogo wanted to keep her for his children, *sim*. But also for himself. He would keep her in the nursery. Keep her in his kitchen.

Keep her in his bed.

Diogo had made up his mind. Marriage was the best—the only—solution for all of them.

He glanced back at the monitor. Watching the tiny flickers of two heartbeats on the ultrasound screen, his own heart enlarged in his chest. He glanced down at Ellie. Her sweet, pale face looked back at him.

"Twins," she said in a low voice. "Can you handle two?"

"I can handle more than that." But two children needed two parents. He opened his mouth to inform her that they would be married today, whether she wished it or not.

Then, looking at her pale, beautiful face, he stopped.

He'd seduced Ellie. Gotten her pregnant. Broken up her wedding and dragged her to Rio. He had completely turned her life upside down.

She was the mother of his children. She deserved his care. So why not be gentle? Instead of bullying her into marriage, why not simply woo her? After all—he smiled to himself—he'd never had any woman resist him for long.

"It's all going to be fine." He reached out to stroke her hair, quelling the impatience in his blood. "You'll see."

Their need to marry was so obvious to him now. He couldn't imagine why she'd turned him down, but he wouldn't let any foolish feminine whims prevent him from doing what was best for all of them. He couldn't.

Tonight, he would give her a chance to catch her breath. Both she and the baby needed a full night's rest. Tomorrow, he'd lure her with all the skill he possessed. Entice her with the romance all women craved. He would convince her. He would persuade. He'd give her a day of romance. One day.

Then, willing or not, Ellie would be his bride.

CHAPTER NINE

Putting aside her pregnancy book and empty pint of strawberry ice cream, Ellie curled up into a ball beneath the bedcovers and stared at the fire in the stark white fireplace. She heard the hard rain patter against the bedroom windows. Days of sunshine, nights of rain. Listening to the dying crackle of the fire and the wind howling outside, she closed her eyes and leaned her head against Diogo's pillow.

Such a strange afternoon.

After the ultrasound, Diogo had taken her out shopping, insisting that she buy whatever would make her comfortable for her stay. She'd actually enjoyed their afternoon together. He'd flirted with her. *And she'd caught herself flirting back.*

Then halfway through the candlelight dinner served by his housekeeper, just as she was tucking into her second plate of lasagna and steamed broccoli, Diogo had gotten a phone call. Without explanation, he'd kissed Ellie on the temple and left her to finish dinner alone!

Staring into the fire, she wondered moodily who'd called him.

Thank heaven she'd had the sense to refuse his marriage proposal. He'd just been trying to alleviate his guilt by pretending to do the right thing. What would he have done if she'd said "yes"? Probably exactly what he was doing now—gone straight to another woman's arms.

It could have been a business call, she told herself. Some late-night problem with the Mongolian iron mine that required a phone call. It could have been business, right? Right?

Yeah, right.

But he had asked her to be his wife. She still couldn't believe it. The playboy of the Western world had proposed to *her*. Who would ever believe it? No one.

So who would ever believe she had *refused* him?

She pulled the bed's comforter up to her ears to keep such unsettling thoughts away. The sheets smelled fresh and clean with a faint scent of his cologne. She closed her eyes, pressing her face against his pillow. She yawned, feeling more exhausted than she'd ever felt in her life.

But she knew she couldn't sleep. Not when, at any moment, he might return and join her in the bed. She yawned. She had to be ready. Ready to fight off not just his seduction, but her own body's traitorous desire.

"Ellie."

Diogo was shaking her. She sat up unsteadily from where she'd been sprawled across the bottom half of his bed. The fire was nothing but ash, and the howling of the wind against the windows had faded.

She realized it was morning. The rain had stopped, and as he opened the shades, she blearily saw the gray-pink hue of dawn across the Atlantic Ocean. She felt disoriented in her rumpled pajamas and messy hair.

Diogo, on the other hand, was fresh and impeccably dressed. He looked crisp and handsome. He'd shaved and changed. He now wore gray slacks, a sharp gray vest and crisp yellow shirt. The elegant cut of his clothes only emphasized the hard-muscled body of the warrior beneath.

She wondered what he'd done last night.

She wasn't jealous, she told herself fiercely. She wasn't even going to ask. He could go out every night with swimsuit models for all she cared. Ellie would, in fact, be glad because it meant he wasn't trying to seduce her.

"Bom dia, amorzão." Diogo held a silver tray. She saw eggs and toast and fruit on a china plate, orange juice in a crystal glass—and a single red rose. "I've brought you breakfast."

She sat up straight in bed. "Breakfast?" she said hopefully as her stomach growled.

But as he leaned over her, placing the tray over her lap, she smelled his woodsy soap on his skin and felt the warmth of his masculine body, and suddenly had to fight hunger for more than just toast.

"Did you sleep well?"

She quickly looked up, hoping he hadn't caught her ogling his backside. "Yes, thank you."

He returned her smile frankly. "How am I doing?"

"At what?"

"At serving you."

She glanced down at the rose on the tray. "You could

probably get a job at a Dairy Burger, if the steel business doesn't work out."

His smile spread into a grin. *"Obrigado."* He opened the napkin and set it on her lap. "I have a busy day planned for us."

"You're not going to work today?"

"No, I am going to show you my city. I want you to love it as I do."

"Why?"

"Does it matter?" He quirked an eyebrow. "Take me up on my offer. Unless, of course, you've already had your fill of billionaire tour guides in exotic foreign cities."

"Well…" It was tempting. She'd certainly always dreamed of traveling as a girl. But…

She took a bite of toast, then resolutely shook her head. "You're not going to change my mind with a little sightseeing, Diogo. After the babies are born, I'm taking them home."

"Home can mean a lot of things. A city. A building." Taking the red rose from the vase on the tray, he gently stroked her cheek with the velvety petals. "Home can mean family."

The sensation of the rose against her skin caused a shiver to spread down her body—then she felt an answering flutter below her heart, even stronger than the one she'd felt yesterday. And this time, she knew. It wasn't her heartbeat.

It was her baby.

She gave a little gasp, sitting straight up in bed, pushing away the rose and the tray and the blankets. She put her hands on her belly. She couldn't feel anything on the outside. But inside…

"What?" Diogo leaned over her with anxiety. "What's wrong? I'll get the doctor."

"No." She felt the flutter again. Tiny, barely noticeable…*but there*. "I felt one of the babies move!"

"You did?" His usual arrogant expression dissipated. He looked strangely unsure of himself.

"Yes." With a delighted laugh, she grabbed his hand and placed it on her belly. "Right here."

He waited. "I don't feel anything."

She moved his hand above her hip bone. "You will." She sighed. "Although it might take a few months."

He looked down at her.

"I can wait if you can," he said quietly.

The air between them electrified. With his hand on her belly, standing over her on the bed, she felt her heart pound. Her eyes dilated. She couldn't breathe.

"I… I won't be your mistress, Diogo," she whispered.

He allowed himself a small, private smile. "I don't want you to be."

He didn't want her anymore?

She should have been relieved, but at his words, a cold pain ripped through her heart. She abruptly released his hand, and the baby fluttered in protest.

I'm not going to ask him where he was last night. I'm not, she told herself fiercely. *I have too much pride….*

"Where were you last night?" she blurted out, then could have kicked herself.

"Where was I?" He tilted his head, looking down

at her. "Only my wife would have the right to ask such a question."

"Any wife of yours wouldn't want to know," she muttered. "She'd probably have a heart attack."

"Ellie." He knelt next to the bed. "You have no cause to be jealous. I was home shortly after you fell asleep."

"Home from where?" Her voice came out an indignant squeak and her cheeks flooded with embarrassment. "And I'm not jealous!"

But of course she was. Desperately. Hopelessly. She'd been heartsick for months, watching from her cubicle as he left his office with one beautiful woman after another on his arm.

And that is exactly how it would be as his wife. He would bed her, pay her bills, give their children a name...but never give her his loyalty or his heart. Her soul would wilt and shrink and die.

She'd promised to stay with him until the babies were born.

Could she survive if he tried to seduce her?

But...could she survive if he didn't?

"Let me show you my city, Ellie," he said softly, taking her hand in his larger one. "You won't regret it."

The desire to hold on to that hand, to be with him as long as she could, overwhelmed every last bit of common sense. Picking up the rose, she climbed out of bed in her long, white cotton nightgown.

"All right," she managed. She glanced down at the red rose still in her hand. It smelled of warmth and summer and happiness. "But we're just going as friends, all right? That's all!"

From the closet, he selected a new dress of stretchy white lace. "Wear this."

"It's lovely." Gathering the dress in her arms, she collected her things to go take a shower. "But just friends, Diogo," she warned. "I won't be your mistress. I mean it!"

"No, you won't be my mistress." The sunlight glinted on the sharp teeth of his smile. "I give you my word."

CHAPTER TEN

FROM THE BASE OF THE towering *Cristo Redentor* statue high atop the jungle of Corcovado Mountain, Ellie could see all of Rio. The stylized Art Deco statue spread his arms wide, embracing all of the city. In the distance, she could see the sharp bookend of Sugar Loaf Mountain rising from the Atlantic.

But as the fragrant breeze whipped her hair around her face, Ellie glanced at Diogo with troubled eyes. Like the statue, he'd been welcoming and warm all day, his arms always reaching out for her. Browsing together though the arts and crafts for sale at the Hippie Market in Ipanema. Buying her a new wardrobe of bikinis, ignoring all her protests as he dragged her into the shop on Copacabana Beach. Taking her for a lunchtime barbeque at a local *churrascaria rodízio*. Traveling to the top of Sugar Loaf Mountain on a cable car.

And every time she glanced at him, his dark eyes were on her. Assessing her. Waiting.

Hot.

Every time their eyes met, it felt like a full-body assault, leaving her breathless. He touched her constantly. Helped her out of the limo. Held her close as they walked through the busy streets.

As she stood beneath the enormous statue and watched the sun finally dropping in the west, painting the white stone the vermillion and orange of sunset, she felt Diogo come behind her. He wrapped his arms around her waist, pulling her back against his body.

A shiver went over her. *Just friends,* she repeated to herself, her teeth chattering. *Just friends*.

"We should go," she whispered.

"Sim," he agreed. "After I kiss you."

"Kiss…?" Her lips parted involuntarily. "But you promised!"

"I never promised not to kiss you." He gently brushed her hair away to nuzzle her neck. "Call it a friendly kiss."

She felt the interested eyes of the few lingering tourists watching them. She turned around in his arms, placing her hands on his chest. She breathed. "Please don't—"

But he lowered his head to hers. It was a hard, hungry kiss, tenderly cradled in his arms, a kiss so powerful and true it was everything she'd once dreamed a kiss could be. On top of the world, with the blue Atlantic and sharp mountains and beauty of Rio de Janeiro at their feet, she felt the colors and faces of the tourists swirl around her in a whirlwind beneath the intensity of his embrace. She almost forgot where she was. Lost in a sensual haze, she hardly noticed the approving smiles and nudges of the tourists around them.

He held her gently, so gently. She felt his hands in her hair, brushing softly against her jawline, holding her as if she were the most precious treasure in all the world.

When he pulled away, he looked down at her. There was an intensity in his dark eyes that made it impossible for her to look away.

"You are hungry, yes?" he whispered.

So hungry. She'd never been so hungry. Her lips trembled. "I..."

He grasped her hand. "Come with me."

His chauffeur drove their shiny black SUV south through the city. In the backseat, Diogo continued to hold her hand. He wouldn't let go. He caressed her with his eyes. As the sky outside darkened into deep shades of scarlet, she felt his heat like a blast of burning sun.

The driver stopped at an elegant restaurant on Ipanema Beach. Diogo helped her from the car, then led her past a line of people waiting outside. The doorman leapt to open the door.

"*Boa noite*, Senhor Diogo!"

The restaurant was full, and yet somehow they immediately got the best table, set outside on the veranda with a view of the red sunset sparkling across waves crashing against the shore. She could see the shadows of the cragged mountains of Rio rising from the mist of sunset.

"You are right," she said quietly, looking out at the view. "The city is like nothing I've ever seen before. Dangerous and beautiful." She looked at him from the corner of her eyes. "Impossible to resist."

He took a sip of his Sapphire martini, then set the sleek blue glass back down on the table. "I'm glad you feel that way."

She glanced down at her plate. Diogo had ordered a classic Brazilian dish for her: *camarão na moranga,* a thick seafood stew with large shrimp with potatoes cooked in coconut milk, served in a small carved pumpkin. It was delicious. She savored every bite. It was truly an experience unlike anything she'd ever had in her life. She looked up.

And so was he…

She took a deep breath as she came to a sudden decision.

"I will stay until the babies are born," she whispered. "I give you my word."

"Tá bom." His eyes swiftly met hers. "That will be best for everyone."

As they left the restaurant after their leisurely dinner, she caught herself in a sigh. "It's been a wonderful day, Diogo." She gave a wistful little laugh. "I'm almost sorry it's over."

He pulled her into his arms, looking down at her with a wicked gleam in his eye. "Nothing is over, *querida*."

"But it's getting so late."

"The night is just beginning."

The old concrete building held the hottest club in Rio—in the most dangerous favela in town. Diogo didn't seem worried, but Ellie knew his bodyguards had insisted on waiting outside. Especially his personal bodyguard, Pedro Carneiro.

Ellie shivered. She always got nervous around Pedro, probably because he looked so much like his brother who'd attacked her in the favela. But Diogo trusted him. And against her will, she was starting to trust Diogo….

He pulled her onto the crowded dance floor. The building was full of gorgeous young Cariocas, all dancing provocatively. The women wore tiny little dresses and little else to hide their curves; the men were strong and brutish, swaying their hips with blatant sensuality. The red lamps illuminated the sweaty, cavernous room as the live musicians began to play an Argentinean tango.

Diogo kissed her hand. But it was no gentlemanly gesture. He kept his eyes leveled on hers, holding her fingers against his own as his lips hotly caressed her skin, and it was a promise of what the night held.

A shiver racked her body.

He won't try to seduce me, she told herself desperately. *He promised.*

But as he pulled her closer into his arms, pressing his hand against the back of her neck, she could not resist him. In rhythm to the music, surrounded by the red light and steam, he held her in continuous contact with his body. Moving against her. Feeling his hard-muscled thigh between her legs, a moan escaped her lips.

He bent his head until it was just inches from her own. Almost close enough to touch. And she wanted him to kiss her. Wanted it badly.

At the last moment, he turned away.

By the time the dance ended, Ellie's body was on fire from her fingertips to her earlobes to her toes. Was it possible to die from wanting a man like this? Could she literally burst into flame, being held against his hard body—but having him not kiss her?

"Just friends," she whispered aloud, closing her eyes. Her breath came in little gasps. "Friends…"

He lifted her chin with a muscular finger, forcing her to meet his eyes.

"I've never wanted to be your friend, *querida*." He ran his hand along the side of her breast to her swelling belly, causing her to shudder from her nipples to her womb. "You are far more to me than a friend."

"I am?" she whispered.

He leaned forward with the sway of the seductive music.

"Marry me, Ellie," he said in a low voice. "I will treat you like a goddess for all your life."

Marry Diogo?

Staring at him, she was tempted more than she could bear. How long had she dreamed of this—of being cherished by Diogo Serrador, the handsome, powerful billionaire she'd admired from the moment she'd become his junior secretary?

It hadn't been a joke yesterday. He truly wanted her as his bride. Ellie Jensen from Flint, Pennsylvania. Of all the women in the world, he'd chosen her to be his love…

His love?

The thought was like a slap in the face.

He didn't love her.

He just wanted to possess her. He wanted the babies to stay in Rio, and he wanted Ellie at his beck and call, in his bed for as long as he wanted her.

This whole day, as beautiful and perfect as it was, had been just one long *setup*.

She squeezed her eyes shut. But even knowing that, she still so desperately wanted to say *yes*….

"What is your answer, *meu amor?*" he asked, stroking her cheek as he looked into her eyes. "Will you make me the happiest of men? Will you agree to be my bride?"

She blinked hard, struggling to regain control. "You don't love me."

"Let me take care of you. Let me keep you comfortable and safe forever." His dark eyes sizzled through her. "Let me give you pleasure such as you've never known."

The longing to surrender poured through her so desperately that her whole body shook with the force of her desire. She wanted to give in. Wanted nothing more than to be the beloved wife of a powerful billionaire who would take care of her and their children for the rest of their lives. Diogo made her skin ignite with every caress. He seared her with every challenging look. And when he smiled…

The word *yes* trembled on her lips. She tried to fight it. She couldn't let him break her heart.

But many playboys grew up and fell in love and were faithful to their wives! she argued with herself. If Diogo didn't love her now, perhaps in time…

His phone vibrated from his pocket, barely audible over the music. He glanced at the phone to see the number of the caller, and the expression on his face changed.

"Excuse me," he told Ellie curtly. Turning away, he spoke warmly into the phone. "Catia…"

And he left Ellie standing alone on the dance floor.

She stood there in shock, surrounded by the pulse of the music and the sexy couples dancing as if they were desperately in love. And her heart melted under the weight of her humiliation.

She'd nearly sold her soul for a kiss.

God, how stupid was she?

Keep her comfortable and safe? Diogo would keep her and the babies like toys on a shelf, for him to take down and play with when it amused him. He would travel the world, run a billion-dollar business, and seduce a new woman every night, and forget all about the family he'd left at home!

He'd interrupted first a kiss—and then his marriage proposal—for the sake of another woman. What kind of fool would agree to be Diogo's wife under those kinds of terms?

No.

She wouldn't let him buy her. Not with his money and not with his sexy charm. She would rather be poor and free than be a rich man's toy. She would rather be a single mother than a miserable, broken-hearted wife!

But it had been so close. After such a wonderfully romantic day, she'd almost agreed to be his bride.

And knowing that, she hardly knew whom she hated more—Diogo or herself.

"I'm sorry." Diogo was suddenly in front of her. "I had to take that call."

"Of course," she said coldly. "I understand. Not that I've ever had a mistress myself."

He stared at her, and she realized part of her was waiting breathlessly, hoping he would deny everything. That small, weak part of her wanted to believe he could be faithful, even by ignoring the evidence of her own eyes.

But he didn't even try to deny it. His lips only separated into a glinty smile. "Right." He reached for her. "Now, where were we? Ah, yes. You were agreeing to marry me."

Humiliation once again rushed through her, leaving her body in flames. She moved before he could touch her.

"You were taking me to the airport," she said evenly. "I want to go home. Now."

"Now?" He stopped, grinding his jaw. His chest rose and fell twice. Their gazes locked as, all around them, couples danced provocatively, grinding their half-naked bodies in movement to the seductive music. "And this is how you keep your promise to remain here until the babies are born?"

Unwilling to trust her voice, she shrugged.

His jaw tightened. She saw him clench his hands.

"*Tá bom.* Just remember, *querida.* You left me no choice."

Without warning, he picked her up in his arms in the middle of the dance floor.

"What are you doing?" she gasped.

"Taking you to our wedding," he growled.

"What? No!" Shocked, she struggled and cried out. The other patrons of the club were so lost in a haze of sex and pleasure and music that they hardly noticed. The few who did notice merely glanced at them with knowing, sly smiles and returned to their dirty dancing.

As Diogo carried her out of the club toward his shiny black Escalade, she tearfully looked up at him. His face was stony, as icy and unreachable as the stars above them.

"Please don't do this!" she begged.

He shoved her into the backseat. "Since you won't

see reason, I have no choice." Diogo climbed beside her and leaned forward to speak to his chauffeur. "Go."

"But—you promised!" she sobbed.

"And unlike you, I never break my word." His handsome face was cold as he looked down at her. "You will never be my mistress. But I swear to you now—*you will be my wife.*"

The night was dark as Diogo's black heart.

Their SUV was covered with mud as they traveled over a rough road into the deep of the jungle. With her window rolled down a crack, she could smell the exotic flowers of the dark forest, hear the eerie howls of spider monkeys and the call of night birds.

Ellie saw a tiny ruined church with peeling white paint that was half-swallowed by jungle.

"I can't marry you," she said desperately. "Please!"

He didn't even glance her way. "It's for the best."

"The best for *you*, you mean."

He turned to her. His eyes were dark, half-hidden in shadow. "I don't understand why you continue to refuse me."

"No, of course you wouldn't!" she said sarcastically. "No woman ever refuses you anything!"

"You are the first." He leaned forward with a frown. "Why? Why do you want our children to be born without a father, without a name? Don't you know the devastation it will cause them? You want me so badly I can feel the heat from your body whenever I draw near. Why do you persist in refusing what we both want?"

"Because… Because I want more!" she cried out.

"More what? More money? More? I do not understand! I offer you what I've never offered any woman." He sounded exasperated, even bewildered. "I've asked you to be my bride."

"You're not asking anything. You're forcing me." She looked away, suddenly fighting tears. "And that should be enough for a woman like me, I suppose. I'm knocked up and have no money, and you're kindly offering to take care of me. I should be grateful, right?"

He ground his teeth. "Enough of this. You won't see reason. *Tá bom*. It doesn't change your fate."

Picking her up in his arms, he carried her into the church.

Five minutes later, the village priest was smiling down at her with kind but bleary eyes, drunkenly swaying on his feet as he spoke the words that would marry them.

At least, Ellie assumed that was what he was doing. It was all in Portuguese.

He turned to Diogo, asking a question.

"Sim," Diogo said with a pleasant nod.

The priest turned to her with the same question.

"No," she gasped out. "No! I won't!"

Looking bemused, the priest turned his red, rheumy eyes questioningly on Diogo. He shrugged with a smile, then turned with a tender expression to his bride. Smoothing his arrogant expression into a smile, Diogo replied to the man in the same language.

"Ah," the priest said with a grin. And he started speaking the ceremonial words again.

"What did you tell him?" she bit out.

"I explained that you're reluctant to marry, due to an innocent bride's blushing modesty."

"I'm standing here in a maternity dress!"

"Fortunately, it's sometimes difficult for a man to tell the difference between early pregnancy and being a bit fat in the waist."

She stiffened. "I wish to God I never let you touch me!"

"Strange, I don't remember that. *Oh my God, my God, don't stop, Diogo*," he said mockingly. *"I love you, I love you, I do!"*

Her cheeks went hot with shame and she wished she could either die—or murder him! "That was a long time ago. I will kill you if you ever touch me again!"

His gaze traced her body in the white lace dress. "A very intriguing proposition," he mused. "Will having you in my bed be worth the risk of death?" His eyes caressed her lips, her breasts. "I think it will."

Self-consciously, she pulled the neckline a little higher over her swelling breasts.

The elderly priest lifted his hand to give benediction on their marriage. Diogo slipped a plain gold band on her finger, and it was finished.

She was Diogo's wife.

Mrs. Serrador.

Married to the man who'd seduced her. Who'd married her without mercy. Who'd stolen her pride along with her heart. Who'd gotten her pregnant with twins.

Who'd made her shiver with desire—who'd once made her love him....

Ellie's teeth chattered as their driver took them from the tiny, remote village on a winding dirt road. She stared out at the mysterious dark jungle, and thought of the life she'd dreamed of having as a girl. Growing up with parents who hated each other and blamed their only child for their wretched lives, she'd been so determined that her life would be different.

But now she'd been forced into marriage, just as they had been. And Diogo would cheat on her, just as her father had done to her mother. He would cheat. Then he would leave....

Ellie covered her face with her hands.

His voice was almost gentle. "Is it really so bad as that?"

She shot her new husband a look full of hate.

"Why have you treated me like this?" she whispered. "What have I ever done to deserve this?"

"What have you done?" He clenched his jaw, looking out into the dark night. "When I was eight years old, my mother dropped me off on the doorstep of a mansion in Barra. She pinned a note to my shirt and told me that I was my father's problem now." He gave her a flinty grin. "She didn't know that he'd died the week before. Or that his legitimate children would have no interest in sharing their home—or their inheritance—with his bastard, who was a living insult to their mother."

Ellie stared at him with her jaw open. She couldn't imagine such a thing—a mother abandoning her child like that! She forgot her anger at Diogo in the onslaught of pity, imagining him as a boy. "They didn't want you to stay?"

"My half sisters had me sent to an orphanage like a prison. There was no food. No clothes. So I ran away." He gave her a hard smile. "Maria Carneiro found me on the streets and brought me home. Her oldest son taught me how to fight. Mateus taught me everything, and I looked up to him as my idol. Until I realized I wanted a different life than any favela could provide."

Looking at Diogo, Ellie couldn't stop herself imagining an eight-year-old boy with a note pinned to his shirt. Bewildered and abandoned. Left on a doorstep for a father he'd never even met, then mocked and unwanted by half siblings. Taught to fight for food in the slums. Without a family, he'd been…

Alone.

No wonder he'd been so determined to make sure his own children didn't suffer the same. In spite of herself, she couldn't help feeling desperately sorry for what he'd experienced as a little boy.

Sorry—for Diogo Serrador? There was a laugh!

She shook her head. "But the whole world believes that you're a Serrador—you attended the best schools and were born with a silver spoon in your mouth!"

"After I made my first million, my half sisters decided to recognize me. I suddenly met their standards, since they'd already squandered their money buying royal European husbands." He glanced out the window. "So I started paying their bills, and they generously awarded me the name of Serrador. Complete with a new biography that they found more flattering to their public image."

"And you forgave them," she whispered.

"Forgave?" He gave her an incredulous look. "It was purely a business decision. I knew my father's connections would be useful. Gold and iron ore are not so different.

Wrestling metal from the earth. Turning it into something that men will die for—that they will kill for." He shrugged. "Taking my father's name accelerated my company's rise. I never planned to have children. I never thought…"

"Thought what?"

Shaking his head, he clenched his jaw. "I won't let any child of mine suffer ever again. Not when I can protect them. Not when I *know*…"

She looked at his taut jawline and cold dark eyes.

"But our babies haven't suffered, Diogo." She timidly reached her hand over his own, pressing it against her belly. "They're safe. See?"

His haggard breathing calmed. The expression in his face lightened.

Then changed.

"Ellie," he said hoarsely. He twisted a tendril of her hair around his finger. "You make me *feel*…"

But he didn't finish the sentence. He lowered his mouth to hers, stroking her tongue with his own and causing heat to rush up and down the length of her body. She wrapped her arms around his body, melting beneath the force of his touch.

As he kissed her, the black SUV barreled swiftly through the dark jungle, pursued by the unearthly cries of birds, the howls of monkeys and the whispered echo of ancient, long-forgotten civilizations.

CHAPTER ELEVEN

ELLIE WOKE WHEN THE Escalade stopped. She realized she'd spent the dark night with her head on Diogo's shoulder, sleeping against him as they traveled over endless bumpy roads.

He looked down at her. "We're here."

"Where?" she said blearily.

The driver opened their door. Diogo took her hand and led her from the mud-splattered Escalade. She felt the warmth and strength of his fingers, felt the scorching heat in his dark eyes. The chauffeur left the suitcase with the discreetly waiting servants and drove down the road in a cloud of dust.

"Bahia. My beach house," he said. "My favorite place in the world."

She saw a luxurious, contemporary beach house set on a sharp cliff over the Atlantic, silhouetted against the orange sunrise. Two sleek stories of glass windows overlooked swaying palm tress and an elegant infinity pool above a private white-sand beach.

"Perfect for a honeymoon," he said softly.

"Honeymoon?" she faltered, but after a night cuddled

up against his body in the backseat of the SUV, she couldn't muster up the strength of her earlier defiance. "No," she tried with more certainty than she felt. "Not going to happen."

"I assure you." He looked down at her in a way that made her shiver. "You are going to be my wife in every way."

He picked her up and carried her over the threshold into the beach house. The rosy light of dawn shimmered through the wide windows, pooling everywhere around her as he set her gently down on the bed. She heard the roar of the ocean crashing outside, felt the fresh, salty tang of the breeze.

He set her down against the mattress and she felt his hands everywhere. He cupped her breasts through her white lace dress.

"You are mine, Ellie," he murmured against her throat. "And I am yours."

"Mine?" she said, her voice choking with emotion. "Just mine?"

He smiled. "While you are in my arms, *querida,*" he promised against her skin, "I am yours."

A feeble bargain, when offered his loyalty of the moment for an eternity of her own fidelity. But beneath his touch she still couldn't protest the injustice. She was lost and adrift in sensation as he stroked her. Every nerve ending hummed with desire.

Only Diogo could make her feel like this.

Her breasts felt full and heavy as he yanked down the stretchy fabric of her dress, suckling her as he cupped the other mound roughly with his hand. She gasped aloud as his lips descended, the erotic pressure of his tongue causing crashes of pleasure in her as tempestuous as the waves against the beach outside.

He slowly pulled off her dress. She was naked on the bed. He pulled off his own vest and shirt and slacks. Standing naked in front of her in the rising sunlight flooding the bedroom, he was illuminated like a Greek god.

"You're beautiful," Ellie whispered, then blushed. She, a married woman and soon to be mother of two, blushed at her own forwardness!

He looked surprised at her compliment. Then he lifted her heavy breasts in his large hands. "And you are magnificent." He kissed slowly down the curve of her body, stopping to give her belly button a sensual lick with the tip of his tongue that made her shiver all over.

Then he stopped, staring down at her belly.

"I'm sorry I got you pregnant against your will," he said in a low voice. "Sorry I had to force you to be my bride. And yet…" He looked up at her, and the stark emotion in his face made her catch her breath. "I find I'm not sorry at all."

Her heart stopped, then started to pound faster. He kissed her, running his hands up and down her hips, her belly, the inside of her thighs. He held her so fiercely, and yet so gently, that she felt lost.

But he did something more. Something that threatened her to the core.

Diogo wasn't touching her as if he callously regarded her like a toy.

He touched her as if he loved her.

And it was doing crazy things to her mind. To her heart. Every caress seduced and lured her into far more than his bed. Every passionate stroke and lick against her flesh seduced her into falling back in love with him. Into a loveless life with a broken, bitter heart and an uncaring, cheating husband.

And yet, she couldn't stop…

Diogo pulled her close against his naked chest, soft with coarse, black hair. She relaxed into his arms, relishing the warmth and protection of his arms.

"Let me love you," he whispered.

He pushed her gently back against the bed. Brushing her hair from her cheek, he pulled off her bra and panties, kissing every inch of her skin as he moved against her.

She tried to fight her desire, but with every stroke against her neck, against her thigh, against the backs of her knees, she was more completely his slave.…

The pleasure was unbearable. She didn't know if it was the pregnancy hormones or the intensity of her engorged breasts, but when he suckled her nipples, her back arched as she desperately pressed against him. He reached his hand between her legs.

She gave an abrupt cry as she felt his fingers inside her. Pressing one thick finger, then two. Languorously, as if he had all the time in the world, he softly stroked her slick wetness, and her whole body tightened as she started to twist beneath his commanding touch.

No. She stared up at the rhythmic swish of the ceiling fan above the bed. She couldn't let Diogo do this. It was one thing to become his wife, or even to share his bed, but she couldn't surrender. Not like this!

Still stroking her with his fingers, he kissed softly up the inside of her thighs. With his other hand, he squeezed her breast.

"Come for me," he whispered hoarsely. She desperately shook her head. She couldn't let herself surrender again. If she did, she would be accepting far more than just pleasure. She would be accepting her fate. She would love him completely, holding nothing back.

"Always so stubborn," he whispered. "We will see who wins."

He lowered his head between her legs. She felt the warmth of his breath between her thighs, felt his fingers stretch her wide. She felt his rough tongue against her core, licking first with the tip and then lapping her with the full breadth of his tongue. And shaking, she could bear it no more. Writhing beneath him, her back arched from the bed as her desperate cry exploded from her lips.

The instant she gasped aloud, he moved. Positioning himself between her legs, he pushed inside her with a slow, deep thrust. For an instant, she felt split apart even as her body shook with impossible pleasure. Then he thrust again. Each was deeper than the last. Her hips moved to join him as he pushed inside her, riding her hard and deep. For Ellie the pleasure was so close to pain that it pushed her higher still, turning her cry of surrender into a scream that she barely recognized as her own.

She felt the muscles of his back tense beneath her touch. He thrust into her one last time with an explosive, triumphant roar. Then he collapsed against her.

It took several long minutes before she came back to earth. She heard the pant of her own breath mingled with his. Felt the slick sweat of their bodies between them. She realized he was still holding her tightly. As if, she thought in wonder, she were a life raft and he was a drowning man.

She looked down at his dark head, his handsome face pressed against her naked chest.

She'd once promised herself then that when she grew up, she would have a marriage of best friends. Of equals. Partners.

This was nothing like those sweet girlish dreams. There was nothing of heaven in this marriage. This was earthy. Dark. Hot. These were the sweaty, physical, real seductions of hell.

And this man…this dark prince who'd stolen every aspect of her innocence…was he a devil? Or something else?

Could she be happy as his wife?

Knowing she shared him with other women? No.

But if by some miracle he could be faithful…

"Diogo…"

He abruptly opened his eyes. "The babies." Immediately, he rolled off her. "Did I hurt them?"

She shook her head. Biting her lip, she hesitated. "I was wondering…"

Did she dare ask her question? *Can you give up your other women, and be faithful to me alone?*

He stretched out next to her on the large bed, supple and satisfied as a well-fed lion. "Come sleep with me." Gently, he pulled her back into his arms to nestle against his chest.

It felt good. Too good. In spite of her fear and jealousy over thoughts of Diogo's other women, she felt herself growing drowsy within the comfort and security of his arms. As she dropped off to sleep in the full brightness of day, she listened to the roar of the surf and the birds calling from beyond the sea.

And she found herself wanting to stay safe in Diogo's strong arms—forever.

CHAPTER TWELVE

ELLIE WOKE HUNGRIER than she'd ever been in her life.

For several moments she listened to Diogo's deep, even breathing next to her. Outside, she could hear the exotic songs of birds in the bright full morning. Then she smiled.

What her husband had done to her since dawn. Multiple times. They'd both been so exhausted, they'd finally fallen asleep in each other's arms....

She blushed. Diogo was her *husband*. The thought astounded her. And what a wedding night—or morning!

Her stomach growled again, more loudly this time. Putting her hand on her belly, she reassured her hungry babies that breakfast was on the way. She climbed softly out of bed and put on an oversized, white cotton robe. Careful not to wake Diogo, she padded into the kitchen. She found peppermint tea in the cupboard and put the kettle on. She stuck some thickly cut bread into the toaster, then slathered both pieces in butter. One piece for each baby. After all, if the babies wanted extra butter and strawberry jam, who was she to deny them their heart's desire?

Smiling broadly, she took her peppermint tea and toast and went outside. Leaving the sliding glass door open behind her, she sat out on the patio to look out at the afternoon sun sparkling across the infinity pool and the ocean beneath the cliffs.

Looking out at the diamond-bright shimmer across the sapphire water, she realized she felt something she'd never expected.

Happiness. Wide, inexplicable joy.

She took a deep breath of the fresh, salty air. The white sand beach was peaceful and the ocean seemed impossibly blue in the hot Brazilian sunlight. A slight breeze swayed the palm trees over the far-off cliffs.

Then she heard the faint buzzing inside the house, rattling hard against the nightstand. The vibrating phone that made her sick to her bones. She heard Diogo's voice, muffled from the bedroom. "Catia?"

Ellie's feeling of happiness and tranquility vanished like smoke.

Her grip tightened over her large ceramic teacup. Catia. Again. Why couldn't the woman leave Diogo alone—not even on his honeymoon?

Even as she told herself she didn't care, humiliation and jealousy surged through her. She glanced down at her plate of toast but she'd utterly lost her appetite. She found herself inching toward the open glass door, straining to hear his low voice.

"*Tchau*," he said, and she heard him getting out of bed.

Ellie hurried away from the door. She struggled not to feel hurt. Not to care. It wasn't like she'd ever expected Diogo to love her. It was merely a marriage of convenience for the babies' sake. She hadn't even wanted to marry him in the first place!

But jealousy stabbed her. It hurt so deep it was impossible to pretend she didn't feel it.

Give up your other women. Be faithful just to me!

Could she ask him? Did she dare?

"There you are." Diogo came through the sliding glass door to stand beside her on the patio. "*Bom dia, my lovely bride.*"

He kissed her briefly on the temple. But looking at him carefully beneath her lashes, Ellie could tell he was tense. He was trying to hide the emotion. He didn't want her to know.

Why? To protect his secret mistress?

"The surf is wild this morning," he observed. He placed his hands on the railing and looked wistfully out toward the ocean.

Carefully setting down her tea on the table, she came up behind him, gently placing her hands on his back. He turned around.

"Who is Catia?" she whispered. "Why does she keep calling you?"

Glancing back at her, his handsome face closed down. "I don't want to discuss it."

"You once said that your wife would have the right to ask."

"Yes." He ran his hand wearily over the back of his head. "Someday I will tell you. But not now."

She felt angry tears spring to her eyes. "You can't honestly expect me to share you!"

He ground his jaw. *"Querida—"*

"Don't call me that! Don't you dare insult my intelligence by pretending you actually care about me!"

"You will share me, Ellie. You have no choice. Just as I will have no choice but to share you."

"I would never—"

"With our children," he interrupted.

She shook her head angrily. "It's not the same thing!"

"I will give you and our babies a good home. You will have untold wealth and the protection of my name. Don't ask more from me. Not yet."

"But I'm your wife!"

His eyes looked dark. "There are some things that a man doesn't discuss with his wife. *Especially* not with his wife."

She shook her head. She couldn't believe that. *Wouldn't* believe it. Why couldn't he just admit he had a mistress and put her out of her misery of wondering? How could they have any marriage at all if they couldn't even be honest?

"Who is she?" she whispered. "Is she beautiful?"

"I'm done discussing this," he said coldly. "Accept that I have my secrets, and be content."

If only she could do that. Pregnant with twins, married to a handsome billionaire, she had everything most women would want. So what was wrong with her? Why couldn't she just be happy, without crying out for his love and fidelity in the bargain?

"Fine," she said in a clipped voice. "Keep your secrets."

"Get dressed." His face was hard as he turned from her. "We must return to Rio immediately."

She gasped at him. "Now? But we just got here! Our honeymoon…"

"Our honeymoon is over," he said. "I have business in Rio."

Yeah, she thought. She could just imagine what kind of business. A vivacious redhead with impossibly long legs, or a sultry, experienced brunette with skills in bed that Ellie couldn't hope to match.

What power did Catia have, that she could so easily make Diogo come at her beck and call? "I don't want to go."

"We leave in five minutes. Be ready." Opening the sliding glass door, he walked back into the house without another glance.

A few minutes later, Ellie was dressed in a loosely fitting white shirt and khaki pants. Feeling desperately sad, she departed the beach house as a trio of laughing maids entered to clean it. Ellie cast one last wistful glance at the bed as the maids stripped the bedlinens. The beach house would soon be immaculate again. As if his wedding night with Ellie had never existed.

Within a day, this beautiful place would be ready to host Diogo's next conquest.

Choking down her bitterness, she followed Diogo toward a waiting helicopter on a flat cliff on the edge of his estate. He barely looked back at her as they walked the hundred yards. Her knees suddenly tottered, and she stopped, hand over her mouth.

As if he somehow sensed her feelings, he turned back. He went immediately at her side. "What is it? Are you sick?"

There was no point in denying it. Not when she likely was green. "I think… I think I'm just hungry. And thirsty. I made some toast, but I didn't eat it…"

Diogo barked out orders to one of his bodyguards. By the time Ellie was seated in the plush leather seat of his Sikorsky helicopter, a maid had brought a freshly made ham-and-cheese baguette, an apple and a bottle of sparkling water.

"Have a good flight, senhora!"

The maid's respect and obvious admiration for Ellie made it clear that she thought Mrs. Serrador very grand— and very fortunate. If only the girl knew the truth!

"If you're still thirsty, there is juice and milk," Diogo said loudly over the noise-muffling earphones. As the helicopter lifted off the ground, he pointed at a small re-frigerator. "And cookies and chips and dried fruit in that box. Once we are home, Luisa will be glad to prepare you a full meal of whatever your heart craves."

"Thank you," she whispered, but there was only one thing her heart truly craved, and he had already turned away from her. For the duration of the short helicopter ride to Rio, he took notes on his laptop, taking business calls on his phone. How could he be so solicitous and kind one moment, then so cold the next?

Because he only cared about the babies, she realized. He wanted Ellie to be comfortable for their sake, but he cared nothing about her feelings. If he had, he wouldn't have abruptly ended their honeymoon after one night to rush back to his mistress!

All the promises his body had made her in bed, every whisper of love in his touch, had been a lie.

She stared down blindly at the passing earth as the helicopter traveled back to Rio. The jungle disappeared, the landscape became more barren. Finishing her sparkling water and apple, she leaned back against her seat and wondered again about the woman. Catia. What kind of woman could hold such power over Diogo?

For the year Ellie had worked for him, Diogo had been known as the uncatchable playboy, the man who would never, ever commit to any woman. The gossipy junior secretaries had kept a gleeful tally of his conquests. The longest record for his undivided attention was held by a Swedish swimsuit model who strutted around Manhattan wearing nothing but hot pants, six-inch heels and teensy-tiny halter tops—in *December*. And even she had only managed to keep his interest for eight days!

If someone like Ebba Söderberg could only last eight days, what qualities must this Catia possess, that with a single phone call she could cause Diogo to bolt across Brazil?

She had to be beautiful…that went without saying. But to capture Diogo, she would have to be more. Sophisticated. Smart. Powerful. She probably had a master's degree in business, spoke five languages, owned a company and traveled in her own jet.

And, of course, she was a wicked temptress in bed. Not like Ellie, who'd only had two nights of sexual experience in her life, both with the same man!

Catia was sexy beyond belief with a perfect figure—not like Ellie, who was rapidly gaining weight and looking lumpier with every passing day of her double pregnancy.

How could Ellie compete with such a perfect woman? She couldn't.

Turning blindly to look out the window, she folded her arms as a rush of emotion threatened to choke her.

Obviously, she'd been delusional on pregnancy hormones to think that because Diogo made love to her, because he'd made her explode with joy, she meant anything to him at all. She'd been crazy to think that because he'd made her his wife, she meant anything to him beyond his children's mother and his own occasional bed warmer.

To him, she was just a knocked-up former secretary who'd never even finished high school, was clueless about designer clothes and had long forgotten her junior-high Spanish. To him, she was simply another possession.

Now that he'd completed his hostile takeover of Ellie, he was already bored and looking for a new challenge.

While she…

As the helicopter descended into Rio, Ellie sucked in her breath.

She was in love with him.

One day as his wife, one night in his arms, and Ellie had fallen in love with Diogo all over again. And though their life together had barely begun, already it was killing her to know that he valued her so cheaply that he would insult and humiliate her like this on the second day of their marriage.

She was still trembling with the realization as they landed on the top of Diogo's office building and took the elevator to the street, where Guilherme waited with the Bentley.

"Leblon," Diogo ordered his chauffeur.

Leblon? As they drove south from the business center of the city, Ellie felt her heart clench. He'd visited that ritzy Rio neighborhood before. During their business trip in February, Diogo had abruptly cancelled a meeting and told the chauffeur to drop him off alone on the Rua João Lira. Distracted with juggling paperwork and her growing attraction for her boss, Ellie hadn't paid attention. She'd been relieved to be left alone for a night at the Carlton Palace to organize the English-language contracts. But now...

Even in February, he'd been seeing this other woman. Catia.

And Diogo cared about Ellie's feelings so little he couldn't even be bothered to hide it.

Her eyes filled with tears as she stared out at the Cariocas playing volleyball across Copacabana Beach. They traveled east into the Ipanema neighborhood past the southern tip of the Lagoa Rodrigo de Freitas. She saw happy young mothers pushing strollers along the edge of the lagoon. Passing into Leblon, all the houses and shops were sleek and gorgeous and new.

But directly behind the new buildings, the slums of the favelas packed onto a hillside, casting a shadow over Leblon's bright beauty.

Diogo was just like Rio. So seductive. So brutal. Did he really expect that she would be so thrilled to be his wife that she'd be willing to turn a blind eye to the ugliness of constant infidelities?

The chauffeur pulled the Bentley to the curb. "*Estamos aqui, senhor.*"

Diogo looked at Ellie for the first time since they'd left Bahia. "Guilherme will take you home."

Ellie looked up at him and fire burned through her, leaving her eyes hot with unshed tears. "Don't leave like this. Please." Her throat felt tight. "Don't go to her."

He looked down at her, his handsome face devoid of expression. "Go home, Ellie."

And he closed the car door behind him.

The chauffeur pulled the Bentley back into the busy Rio traffic. Turning around, Ellie looked through the back window as they drove away. She saw Diogo go up a flight of stairs to knock on the bright red door of a town house. A beautiful brunette flung open the door with a beaming smile. Taking his hand in her own, she pulled him inside.

And cold rage such as Ellie had never felt in her whole life swept through her. Fury swept through her body, freezing her heart into stone, congealing her spine into steel.

How dare he?

"Stop this car." Turning to the chauffeur, she said more loudly, "Stop this car!"

"No, Senhora Ellie," he replied, giving her a nervous smile in the rearview mirror. "The senhor, he ordered me to take you home—"

Her heart was pounding so furiously she thought she'd explode if she didn't tell Diogo exactly what she thought of him—and that little brunette of his, too. All right, so maybe Ellie wasn't the most glamorous or wealthy or well-educated woman in the world, but she didn't deserve to be tossed aside like a bag of chips!

"Fine," she growled. "Don't stop!"

As the car still moved, Ellie flung open her door. With a horrified gasp, the chauffeur slammed on the brakes in the crawling rush-hour traffic.

She ran through the honking cars for the curb. Panting, red-faced with anger, she ran up the exact same stairs she'd seen Diogo climb.

She pounded on the door.

Once.

Twice.

The door opened. The same beautiful brunette answered. She was every bit as lovely, mysterious and irresistible as Ellie had feared.

She spoke with an upper-crust British accent as she looked Ellie up and down scornfully. "What do you want?"

"You must be Catia." Ellie drew herself up with all the blue-collar pride of the generations of steel workers and coal miners that ran in her veins. She stalked past her husband's mistress with her chin held high. "Tell Diogo Serrador that his wife is here."

CHAPTER THIRTEEN

"ELLIE." DIOGO'S FACE became instantly angry as he rose to his feet. He'd been sitting back on the sofa, looking far too comfortable in the brunette's cozy little house. As if this place were his home!

"I won't share you!" she ground out. "I won't!"

His brows lowered furiously. "*Maldição*, I won't be spied on like this—not by you or anyone!"

"You expect me to just accept whatever story you give me?" she demanded, perilously close to tears. "You think I should be quiet and grateful and put up with you cheating on me? I won't!" Her hands clenched into fists. "I'm your wife, I have feelings, and I expect you to— I expect—"

What did she expect?

I expect you to be true to me as I'm true to you.

I expect you to love me, as I love you.

God, she was a fool!

"Damn you," she whispered, sinking into the couch as she struggled to hide her sobs. "Damn you to hell."

In an instant, he crossed the room. He held her in his arms with unexpected tenderness. He kissed her temple softly, stroking her hair.

"She's not my mistress, Ellie," he said. "She's not."

"But—"

His eyes were dark with emotion. "I would not have married you if I intended to betray you."

She looked at him, afraid to believe the words she desperately wanted to believe. "Then what are you doing here?"

He shook his head, tightening his jaw. "I didn't want you to know. I was…ashamed."

"Ashamed?" she gasped. "Of what?"

"Know this." Raising her chin, he forced her to meet his eyes. "When I forced you to take my name, I gave you my loyalty. I will never break my promise. Never."

She shook her head tearfully. "But it's not a real marriage."

Lowering his lips, he kissed her, a hot embrace that made fire rush through her veins.

"Tell me that's not real," he demanded.

Ellie heard a startled squeak from the doorway. Dazed, she looked up to see the brunette standing in the doorway holding a tray. The woman was staring daggers at Ellie. If she wasn't Diogo's mistress, she obviously wished to be.

Ellie turned back to Diogo. "So why— Why are you here with Catia," she asked in a small voice, wanting desperately to believe, "if she's not your mistress?"

"Ah." He followed her gaze to rest on the brunette. "Her name is Angelique Price. She's a nanny."

"Nanny?" she repeated numbly. As if on cue, she heard a sharp, rhythmic bang against the hardwood floor as a little girl, about five years old and holding a doll, ran into the room. She stopped, looking at Diogo with big, frightened eyes.

"What are you doing here?" the little girl said in tremulous English, clutching her doll. "Go away. I don't want you here!"

Diogo rose steadily to his feet. "Hello, Catia." He took a step toward her. "I've missed you, *minha pequena*. Angelique called and said you were asking for me. I came as quickly as I could."

"No! I don't want you! Go away!"

Diogo picked the child up in his arms. Her doll dropped with a crash to the floor as he hugged her close, whirling her around the room, but instead of bursting into childish squeals of laughter, she howled, "No! Put me down! I don't want you here, don't want you!"

She was not a pretty little girl, except in the sense that all children are beautiful. Her hair was mousy brown. She wore thick glasses, her teeth were crooked, and she was far too thin and serious for a five-year-old child. Ellie's heart went out to the girl.

Then her plain brown eyes fixed on Ellie.

"Who is that?"

He stroked her hair tenderly. "That is Ellie. My wife." He turned. "Ellie, I'd like you to meet Catia," he said quietly. "She's my daughter."

An hour later, after the little girl went into the kitchen to have lunch with her nanny, Ellie and Diogo sat on the sofa in the front room. The visit between Catia and her father had not improved, in spite of all Diogo's trying.

The more he'd attempted to charm and please the little girl, the more she'd howled and pushed him away.

"I hired Angelique through an agency. I never even knew I had a daughter till this past Christmas," he told Ellie, rubbing his head wearily with his hands. "*Maldição,* she lived in Rio all these years, but I never knew."

"Where is her mother?" she asked softly.

His dark eyes looked haunted. "She's dead."

"Dead?"

He clenched his jaw. "Yasmin was a dancer—so passionate, so full of life. When I met her, I was building a new mine in Saskatchewan. We only had a few dates a few weeks apart. On our third date, she asked me to marry her. I thought she was a gold digger trying to pin me down. So I didn't ask questions. I just left her." He looked away, staring at the gleam of the hardwood floor. "When I told her she meant nothing to me, she said she was done with me. She said she loved someone else too much to waste any more time with me. It never occurred to me that she might be pregnant."

She stared at him, her mouth agape. "Oh, Diogo," she whispered.

"After I found out about Catia, I couldn't stand the thought that I'd unknowingly abandoned my daughter for five years. I had to make sure that no other woman could get pregnant without my knowledge…"

"So you had a vasectomy."

He nodded wearily.

She swallowed. It all made sense. "What happened to Yasmin?"

He clawed his hair back. "She tried to support her baby alone, but couldn't do it after she got injured. I found out later she tried to contact me when Catia was six months old. She sent me a letter. But I never got it. Wright saw to that. He threatened her."

Her jaw dropped. "Timothy?"

His lips flinched into a humorless smile. "Yes."

"Timothy?" she gasped. "Threatened the mother of your child?"

"When I found out at Christmas, he told me he was protecting me. He wrote Yasmin a letter informing her that if she ever tried to contact me again, he would have her arrested for extortion." He clenched his jaw grimly. "Instead, he offered to buy the baby from her for ten thousand dollars."

She gaped at him. "Ten thousand dollars!"

"She was terrified he would steal her child from her, so she never tried to contact me again. But with no family or means of support, she ended up working in Rio as a high-class hooker." He looked up at her with hollow eyes. "And that's how she died. One of her clients beat her to death at Christmas."

Ellie sucked in her breath, hardly able to comprehend the horror of it. "And Catia?"

He shook his head. "Yasmin always sent her to a babysitter when she entertained clients. Catia knows that her mother is dead, but not how she died."

"Thank God," Ellie said devoutly. "That poor child…"

It was all such a tragedy. Ellie had worked herself into a jealous frenzy over a beautiful mistress who had just been a figment of her imagination.

All along, her rival had been a motherless child.

"Don't worry," Diogo said coldly, misreading her pause. "I understand that Catia is my child, not yours. Whatever you think of my unreasonable expectations of a bride, I do not expect you to help me raise her."

Ellie straightened on the sofa.

"Nonsense," she said crisply. "She's your daughter. She must live with us."

His eyes widened.

"You would…do that?" he said stiltingly.

"Of course!" She frowned. "What I don't understand is why she's still living in this house with a nanny. Why hasn't she been living with you since you got custody?"

"I work such long hours, and travel so often to New York. I thought it better to let her stay in her home…"

She stopped him with a look. "In the home where her mother was beaten to death?"

"You're right, you're right." He clenched his fists, pressing them against his eyelids. "The truth is, I want her with me. Every day. But she refuses to leave this place. When I try to pack up her things to take her, she screams bloody murder and clings to Angelique."

"I don't like that woman, Diogo. I don't trust her." *She wants you for herself,* she added silently.

"Catia has lost her mother. She doesn't know me. And I just can't get through to her." He leaned his head in his hands. "I thought if I gave her a few months to grieve, she would be willing to accept her new life as my daughter. Now I'm at the end of my rope. I don't know what to do. Aside from inviting Angelique to live with us, as well."

Angelique—living with them? She stared at him, aghast. "You just need to be firm."

"Be firm?" He gave her a gaunt smile. "With a five-year-old child? Drag her kicking and screaming from her home? I haven't the heart, Ellie. I can't do it." Sounding weary, he added beneath his breath, "God help me, I don't know what to do."

She stared at him for a moment. Gently, she reached over and stroked his dark hair. He looked utterly beaten. Diogo Serrador, the barbarian of Wall Street and scourge of the steel industry, looked defeated and destroyed.

Ellie stroked his head. Closing his eyes, he gave a sigh, turning his cheek toward her caress.

She had to do something. She couldn't bear to see him suffer like this. Or the poor child, either. She had to fix this. Had to make them whole again.

"I am going to help you," she said steadily.

Diogo opened his eyes to look at her. His expression looked so vulnerable. Strikingly boyish. And she realized that he blamed himself for everything. For Yasmin's death. For his daughter's pain. The child he hadn't even known existed until a few months ago...

"What will you do?"

She kissed him softly on the forehead. "I'll go talk to her. It's going to be all right, Diogo," she said. "I promise."

The terrible hope in his eyes as he watched her go almost broke her heart.

She went down the hall to the kitchen, but didn't find either Catia or her nanny. Frowning, Ellie went upstairs. She stopped when she heard voices behind a bedroom door.

"Your daddy doesn't love you," she heard Angelique say. "He's just like the other bad man I told you about, the one who hurt your mama. I'm the only one who can keep you safe. If you let him take you from the house, he will hit you and yell. Unless I'm with you. So just remember—don't leave here without me! And then—" her voice changed, becoming calculating "—I'll marry him and never have to work again…"

The little girl said something so softly that Ellie couldn't hear. The nanny gave a hard snort.

"Oh—her. She's not your new mommy. But don't worry. We'll soon be rid of her."

Ellie threw open the door. She saw a smug nanny and tearful child, and fury went through her to her bones.

"What are you telling her?" she demanded.

"What do you mean?" Angelique said with an innocent smile. "Just telling her to be a good girl for her father. Shall we go down now for lunch, madam?"

Ellie grabbed the other woman's wrist. "You horrible, horrible woman. You—are *fired*."

"Fired!" Real fear went through her eyes. "You can't fire me! Only Mr. Serrador can do that!"

"Get out!" Ellie shouted, and the woman ran. "Get out before I hit you with my shoe!"

Catia gave a terrified little squeak, and Ellie fell on her knees in front of her. "It's all right, sweetie," she said gently. "It's all right. Angelique was just being mean. And wrong. Your father loves you. He would never, ever hurt you!"

She tried to give her a hug, but the girl shrank back with a fearful gasp. Poor Catia really believed every evil lie that Angelique had told her. Desperately, Ellie said, "We want you to come home with us, to stay—"

"No!"

Tears filled her eyes at the motherless child's confusion and grief. She took a deep breath, praying for a way to reach her. "We want you with us. You'll have your very own room. Lots of toys, and—"

"No!" she shrieked. "I won't go!"

"And siblings," Ellie continued desperately, hardly knowing what she was saying. "A baby brother and sister to play with very soon..."

The shrieks abruptly ended.

Staring at her, Catia sucked in her breath with a hiccup. Ellie was afraid to say a word to break the spell.

"Babies?" the girl finally whispered. "A brother and a sister?"

Ellie nodded. She put her hands on her loose white shirt, showing off her gently swelling belly. "Your father and I are going to have twins, Catia. In early November."

"But...then...why do you want me?" she asked falteringly.

Blinking back tears, Ellie stroked her dark hair. "The babies need a big sister to show them how to play."

"Oh," Catia breathed with longing. "I can do that. I can show them how to play with a ball, and ride a bike, and lots of things..."

"I know you can." Ellie held out her hand. "We want you in our family, Catia. We love you. We need you."

"You do?" The girl looked up timidly.

"Yes!" Tears were running down Ellie's face and she didn't even try to wipe them away. Within hours, she'd already come to love this motherless girl who desperately wanted to belong, to be safe, to be loved. Just as Ellie once had….

Holding her breath, Ellie waited, hand extended.

Tentatively, Catia placed her small hand in her own.

Joy flooded Ellie's heart. "You won't be sorry," she whispered. "I promise. You'll always be safe and happy with us."

Together, they walked down the stairs.

In the salon, she saw Angelique Price making her case to Diogo, who was standing by the fireplace with a hard expression. But having once seen his heart, Ellie now realized that unfeeling arrogance was just the mask he wore over a heart that felt too much.

A heart just like her own.

"Your new wife is jealous of the child, Mr. Serrador," the beautiful nanny was pleading, putting her graceful hand on his arm. "She's crazy! Don't let her take the child from me. I think she intends to do the little girl some harm. She's trying to get rid of me so she can send Catia off to boarding school—or worse. If you love your daughter, for God's sake, don't let her fire me!"

They both looked up as Ellie and Catia came down the stairs. Diogo's face lit up in astonished wonder at the sight of his daughter holding Ellie's hand.

"I'm ready, Papa," the little girl said shyly. "I want to go home to our family."

"Oh, *pequena*," he gasped.

She held out her thin arms. Diogo raced halfway up the stairs and took the little girl in his arms. This time, there could be no doubting the brilliance of her smile.

"After all," she chirruped happily, "someone has to teach those babies how to play!"

He hugged the child fiercely, looking at Ellie over her shoulder.

"Thank you, Ellie," he whispered, and there were tears in his eyes. "Thank you."

"She can't be trusted," Angelique howled shrilly. "Who are you going to believe, her or me?"

With his free hand, Diogo took his wife's hand in his own.

"I believe my wife fired you," he said coolly. "You have five seconds before I toss you out the door."

"You wouldn't."

He took a step toward her, and Angelique fled.

Diogo turned back to his little family.

"Come," he said tenderly. "Let's go home." He kissed the back of Ellie's hand. And in his dark eyes, she saw a new warmth—and beneath it, the promise of fire.

CHAPTER FOURTEEN

I'm going to take her from you.
DIOGO STARED DOWN AT the note in his hands.

He'd shrugged off the notes at first. The first one, in his briefcase when he returned from a business trip to New York in early June. The next on his private plane in September. Now this one, tucked in the car that his wife and daughter used in Rio.

Guilherme swore he didn't know how the notes got into the Bentley, and Diogo believed him. So how had they gotten there?

But he already knew who'd sent them, knew it down to his bones. Timothy Wright. The ruined lawyer had gone underground, hunted by the American police—and now apparently determined to take his revenge against the former boss who'd given evidence against him.

How was Wright leaving notes like this, in Diogo's private, protected world? In spite of all his bodyguards? Was the man a ghost—a demon?

I'm going to take her from you.
Diogo crumpled the note in his hands and tossed it into a trash can on the street outside the Carlton Palace.

His men would track Wright down. But why was it taking so long? Diogo couldn't protect his family if he couldn't find his enemy. He'd had enough, he thought with a growl. It was time for him to call all his men—and call in some favors.

He wanted the bastard *found*.

Getting out of the elevator on the ninth floor, he gave his waiting bodyguards instructions. Pedro promised he'd take extra care, but Diogo was still tense as he pushed open the door into the penthouse.

Two pairs of feminine eyes looked up at him happily from the kitchen. Catia wore a fancy pink dress and a tiara. Next to her, Ellie was heavily pregnant, gorgeous and radiant wearing a simple black knit maternity top and straight-legged pants.

"Papa, you're home just in time!" Catia chortled. "I made dinner all by myself!"

He raised an eyebrow, glancing from his pretty, glowing wife to his daughter. Ellie was due to have the babies any day, while Catia had really blossomed from the five months in her care. Her young face sparkled beneath her tiara.

"Dinner smells delicious," he told her. "I've never had a princess cook my dinner before!"

"Oh, Papa. The dress isn't for cooking your dinner," the little girl giggled. "I'm a princess for Beatriz's party!"

Diogo dimly recalled that a Brazilian general's daughter was having a slumber party for several friends from their private school. Halloween was increasingly celebrated in Rio—Cariocas always on the lookout for another excuse for a party.

"Do you like my tiara?" Catia reached up on her head to touch it. "Mom and I glued on the rhinestones ourselves!"

"It was fun," Ellie said, hugging the little girl and tousling her hair affectionately. She glanced up at Diogo with a sudden laugh. "Oh, I just spoke with my grandmother…"

"Yes?" he said innocently.

"She got the birthday present you sent, and she's the envy of all her friends. You really don't fool around when you give presents, do you?"

"The grandmother who raised you deserves the best."

Ellie's blue eyes glowed. "I can't imagine what possessed you to send a seventy-year-old woman a yellow Ferrari, but she's been joyriding all over Pennsylvania."

"I saw that orange lipstick, and knew it would take a lot to impress her."

"Gran says she's never had so much fun in her life. She really wants us to move back." She paused. "She sent me a link to all these great schools in New York…"

Not this old argument again. Irritated, he shook his head. "There are good schools *here*."

"I know. I know. But New York…" Her voice trailed away wistfully.

"Mom!" Catia wailed. "It's burning!"

Ellie helped her stir the sauce, then handed Diogo the spoon. He tasted it with gusto. *"Estava delicioso! Meus cumprimentos ao chefe."*

"My compliments to the chef," Ellie translated easily.

"Your Portuguese is improving!"

"Obrigada," she said with a grin. "I've had a good

teacher." Ellie's eyes met his over the stove impishly. "By the way, I let Luisa have the night off," she said with studied innocence. "While Catia's at her slumber party, I'm afraid we'll be all alone…"

"We will, eh?" The sexy, mischievous look in her eyes sent a thrill through his body. Even at nearly nine months pregnant, she was the sexiest woman in the world to him. They made love every night. And with Catia at her friend's house, the whole evening stretched before them, hours and hours to laugh and play in the most adult way possible…

I'm going to take her from you.

His jaw clenched. He looked over the penthouse with critical eyes. Ellie had made many changes over the last few months. The white walls, hard furniture, and steel-and-glass artwork were all gone. The walls were now a creamy yellow. The tables were glossy wood with bowls of flowers, and the sofas were plush and comfortable. Pictures of their family, of Catia in front of the Statue of Liberty on a recent trip to New York, of the three of them laughing together at the beach house last month, now lined the walls.

It felt like his home in a way it never had before. He loved it anew. Not because of the large windows and gorgeous view, but because of Catia…and Ellie.

But the windows are too large, he thought now with a scowl. Even with the bodyguards outside and on the floor below, the building had the public access of a hotel. Security might be breached. It was too vulnerable by half.

He had to find Wright. *Now.*

"I'll be back," he told Ellie abruptly.

"What's wrong?" she said, looking at him with piercing eyes.

Maldição, he had a hard time lying to her. But he wanted her greatest concern to be shopping for baby clothes and playing with Catia. Not worrying about some crazed man from their past who wished them harm.

It wasn't that he thought Ellie was too weak to deal with it. On the contrary. He'd realized her strength when he saw her coming down those stairs in Leblon holding Catia's hand. She'd achieved the impossible that day— done something that Diogo could not do no matter how hard he'd tried.

She'd brought their family together.

In many ways, he thought, his wife was far more powerful than he was. Bearing children, giving constant unconditional love, being the emotional heart of a home—they all demanded strength and courage that most men, including Diogo, couldn't possibly comprehend.

But protecting them was *Diogo's* job.

"Nothing's wrong," he said evenly. "Everything is fine."

Turning away before she could ask more questions, he went to his study and got on the phone. He called in some favors from friends in various government agencies, including Interpol. But hanging up the phone, he still felt unsettled.

His men would find him, Diogo told himself, but he was distracted all throughout dinner. After the delicious meal, he hugged Catia farewell and Pedro, his most trusted bodyguard, carried her little suitcase and accompanied her to the waiting car downstairs. The general's compound was notoriously tight with security; Diogo knew that Catia would be safe there.

"I can tell something's bothering you." He felt Ellie's arms wrap around his waist. "You might as well just tell me. Don't make me lure it out of you," she said teasingly.

He turned to face her and growled, "My only problem is that it's been too long since we've been alone together."

Pulling her into the bedroom, he made love to her with almost frantic intensity, ripping off her clothes, pulling her over him, thrusting inside her deeply as she rode him until they both were sweaty and gasping. Then he held her all night. She slept cradled in his arms. But for him, sleep was impossible. He stared up at the ceiling, then rose from bed before first light.

"Where are you going?"

He'd thought she was still asleep. He looked at her on the bed. She was leaning back against the pillows, naked from the waist up, looking so impossibly lush and beautiful that it made his heart hurt.

He clenched his jaw. "I need to get to work. The Vahlo acquisition…"

"Forget work," she grumbled good-naturedly. "Stay home with me and play."

"The sure way to the poorhouse."

"I think we could manage with a few million less."

"It's Wright," he heard himself blurt out. "He's threatening to take you from me."

To his surprise, Ellie just laughed aloud. "Timothy? Of course he wants me. At nine months pregnant, I'm so very beautiful, so irresistible to men," she teased.

"You *are*," he insisted. He leaned over her on the bed, kissing her lips softly. "He's sent me anonymous notes."

"If they're anonymous, how do you—"

"I know," he said grimly. "And I should have killed him when I had the chance. Until he's caught, you must never leave the penthouse without Pedro. Do you understand me?"

She shook her head, then reached out to playfully muss his hair. "Why don't you just admit it?"

"Admit what?"

She looked him straight in the eye. "You love me."

He stared at her. Sweat rose to his forehead. "What?"

She sat up straight on the bed. "You love me, Diogo. Just as I love you. I've been in love with you for ages. I think since the first time you called me into your office, demanding for me to take a memo on the Trock deal."

His jaw clenched and he stood back from her. The intimate mood was suddenly gone.

Love her?

Love was for women who didn't know better.

Love was for men who were too weak to control themselves.

Love made a man stupid. Made him vulnerable. Left him helpless.

And he couldn't be helpless. Not with so much at stake.

"You love me," Ellie whispered. Her clear blue eyes met his. "Please. I need to hear it. All these months, I've been waiting and praying to hear it. I thought that if I showed my love for you in a thousand small ways, giving you a loving home, you would know—"

"Ellie, I can't deal with this now." His whole body felt tense as he turned away. "I need to take a shower."

"Diogo?"

He turned on her fiercely. "I don't love you, all right?"

She went pale. She licked her lips, tried to speak, couldn't.

"I *don't*," he insisted. "And if you love me, I'm very sorry. I never wanted your love. We have a partnership, *querida*. A friendship. An intense connection in bed. A wonderful family. That's all. But for God's sake, that should be enough!"

"I don't believe that," she responded passionately. "The way you kiss me. The way you want to protect me…"

He abruptly left the bedroom, heading toward the bathroom. "I need to get ready."

He took a thirty-second shower and quickly got dressed. When he came back, he saw her sitting on the sofa in the front room, wrapped in his robe. Dawn was flooding the room with soft pink light. She was hugging herself, staring down at the floor.

Something lurched deep inside his heart.

"Ellie…" He took a deep breath. "We can talk more later."

"Right," she said dully. "Later."

Ellie didn't look up as he left. He would deal with her later. Right now, he had more pressing concerns. He went to his modern office building on the Avenida Rio Branco. He met with Andrew MacCandless, his company's chief of international security, then got reports on Wright's most recent sighting yesterday— traveling to São Paulo from New York on a borrowed plane. He'd apparently promised a wealthy childless couple on Park Avenue that they would soon receive newborn twins for the price of four million dollars.

Newborn twins.

I will find him, Diogo told himself with a haggard breath. He told his chief of security to bring in a private army if that was what it took. The man was threatening his family. He had to be brought down.

Just as the man grimly left to execute his orders, his secretary spoke in Portuguese over the intercom.

"Your wife is here, sir."

"Here?"

"I just got the call from downstairs reception. Shall I have them send her up?"

He paused. He didn't want to see Ellie now. There was no point in talking. She loved him, and he didn't love her.

Seeing her pain killed him. *Distracted him.*

Still…

Ellie had never come to his work before. He couldn't turn her away. "Send her up."

As he paced his office waiting for her to arrive, he couldn't stop thinking about her. His beautiful, warm wife, the mother of his children. He couldn't stand the thought of anyone threatening to take her from him.

Diogo had known what Wright was capable of. Why had he let the man go?

If anything happened to Ellie, it would be Diogo's fault.

He clenched his hands. He couldn't let anything happen. He wouldn't. He would die first.

He loved her.

The stealthy thought brought him up short.

He loved her?

It was true she had changed his life completely. His existence had once been cold. Going from one woman to the next, filling his life with business deals and empty pleasures, he hadn't realized at the time how miserable he'd been—or how alone.

But Ellie had changed everything. She'd turned his cold house into a home. Taught his daughter to love and trust again. Made his whole life bright with color and rich and warm. Somehow he'd come to value her opinion and her strength more than anything…

Was that love?

He couldn't go to sleep at night without making love to her. He couldn't get out of bed in the morning without kissing her and seeing her bright face. He couldn't imagine coming home if not to her….

Maldição. He was in love with his wife.

How was it possible that he hadn't known?

How was it possible it had taken him so long to realize that he'd gotten everything all wrong? Love wasn't to be feared. It didn't leave a man vulnerable. To the contrary. Knowing that he loved her, and she loved him back, made him more fearless and determined than he'd ever been in his life….

He heard a knock at the door. His wife entered, her face wan and pale.

"Ellie." He went to her immediately, reaching for her, desperate to hold her in his arms. "*Meu amor.* I'm so glad you're here. I have to tell you—this morning, when I—"

She backed away. "Don't touch me."

He froze in place, unable to look away from her

face. Her expression was so distant and strange. Not like Ellie at all.

"I've come to say goodbye," she said. "I'm leaving."

"What?" he whispered.

Her china-blue eyes crackled like frozen ice beneath the sea. "You've made it clear you'll never love me. So I'm going home. Back to New York."

"No." Grabbing her fiercely, he looked down at her. She wouldn't leave. She couldn't. Not now—not when he finally had realized he loved her!

"Ellie, you have to listen," he said hoarsely. "I should never have said those things to you this morning—"

"I'm glad you did," she said, cutting him off. "It was time I faced the truth."

"You are my wife. Pregnant with my children." He swallowed. "I do not want you to leave. Ever."

She looked away miserably. "I have no choice."

"But, Ellie, I…" He took a deep breath. *I love you.* He licked his dry lips, and tried again. "I…" But unlike when he proposed, these strange words stuck in his throat. "You do have a choice," he whispered. "I'm not ordering you to stay. I'm asking you," he said in a low voice. "Please. Stay. For me."

She shook her head, and he saw tears in her eyes. "I can't." She wrenched away. "I want a divorce."

"A divorce?"

His hands clenched on empty air. He could barely breathe over the enormous lump in his throat. "But—why?"

"I'm in love with someone else."

He sucked in his breath. "Who?" he demanded fiercely.

"Timothy," she whispered.

He gaped at her, not understanding.

"You never treated me like I wanted," she said. "You never bought me flowers or read me poetry. You don't know anything about love. Timothy does. He's the man I want."

Every word she spoke was like a stab in his body. He felt every slice of the knife keenly. Down to the bone.

Then anger rushed through him. "Timothy Wright is a monster. You could not possibly love him."

"But I do." She blinked rapidly. "We can share custody," she offered. "The babies will have your last name. But I will have my divorce."

"No." He grabbed her angrily, his hand gripping her arm hard enough to bruise. "No, Ellie, damn it, no! I won't let you go!"

"You're hurting me!"

Hurting her? It was nothing compared to what she'd done to him. But when she winced beneath his grip, he let her go.

"Timothy Wright will never come near my children," he bit out. "He's made a fortune over the last two years ruining innocent lives. I will not allow mine anywhere near him."

Her eyes widened. "I will protect them—"

"You? You can't protect anyone. You're every bit as weak as I first thought. No loyalty to your children, or to..." *Or to me.* A new thought rushed through him, almost too painful to bear. "What do I tell Catia?" he said, barely able to speak over the jagged pain in his throat. "What am I to tell her—that another mother has left her?"

"Tell her…" Ellie closed her eyes in pain. "Just tell her I love her. And that all I wanted to do was to keep her safe."

"No." He couldn't believe this was really happening. Anguish ricocheted through him, cutting more savagely than he'd ever been hurt before. "You're my wife, Ellie. We need you." He took a deep breath. "*I* need you."

"Diogo—"

Sweeping her up in his arms, he showed her his heart with a powerful kiss. It was a deep kiss, fierce and true, and tangy with the salt of her tears. Her large belly was between them, creating a perfect circle of family.

When he pulled away, he searched her face, desperate for a sign of everything he'd come to love and trust.

But her eyes remained closed, as if she were trying to savor this kiss forever.

"And me?" he whispered. "What do you have to say to me?"

She finally opened her eyes, shining with tears. "All I have to say to you is—goodbye."

With an audible growl, he opened his mouth to tell her that he had no intention of letting her go. She was his wife. The mother of his children. He would force her to stay. She belonged to him.

Then he realized: Ellie didn't belong to him.

They belonged *together*.

If she wanted to be free, he couldn't force her to stay. He couldn't chain her to the bed. He couldn't ignore her feelings for the sake of his own. Not anymore.

He loved her.

Diogo took a deep breath, struggling to get his old power back. To pick her up and toss her into the Bentley.

To drive her home and kiss her senseless. To lock her up and force her to stay until she saw sense.

But he couldn't.

A hard Brazilian curse fell silently from his lips. Love had made him weak, just as he'd always feared.

Without Ellie, they would not be a family. Without her, he lost everything he'd come to love.

But because he loved her, he had no choice but to let her go.

His hands clenched. "Until the babies are born, Pedro will constantly be at your side," he said coldly. "After that, you can do whatever the hell you want. I'll give you your divorce."

She shook her head. "Pedro is already waiting for me."

"Good," he choked out. He turned away as tears pricked the back of his eyes. "*Sai fora,* Ellie. I'm sick of the sight of you. Don't leave Rio. My lawyer will be in touch."

Her whole body went tense at the word *lawyer.* She turned to go, then stopped at the door. Without meeting his eyes, she spoke her final words.

"Goodbye, Diogo," she whispered. "I will always love you."

He sat heavily down at the desk after the door closed. He sank his head in his hands. He'd been stupid to give his heart. It had all been a trap. All the warmth and comfort and trust and love had been nothing but an illusion to make him weak. To make him believe...

He'd trusted her. *Loved her.* And he'd been so sure she loved him in return.

I love you. He still remembered the way Ellie's face

had glowed that morning when she spoke the words, as if alight with the brilliant fire of the Brazilian sun. *I thought that if I showed my love for you in a thousand small ways, giving you a loving home, you would know.*

He pressed his knuckles hard against his closed eyes. He'd been a fool. She'd never loved him, really. It had just been...

It just...

It just...didn't make sense.

He slowly opened his eyes.

Just tell her I love her, Ellie had whispered. *And that all I wanted to do was to keep her safe.*

Catia.

He snatched up his phone from his desk. Pacing back and forth across his office, he called first Ellie's cell phone, then Pedro's. No answer. He called security downstairs and was informed that Mrs. Serrador and the bodyguard were long gone.

Diogo's hands shook as he called his men at the hotel. None of them answered, even though he let it ring. Finally, he called his chief of security and got an answer.

"I just reached the Carlton Palace, Mr. Serrador," the Australian said grimly. "It looks like someone knocked out all the bodyguards by putting something in the coffee. No one died, but I just found Guilherme stuffed into a utility closet on the back staircase. He's barely breathing—looks like he was chloroformed from behind. Ambulance is on the way."

"And Catia?" Diogo demanded, barely able to breathe.

"Haven't seen her, Mr. Serrador," MacCandless replied. "We're searching the building. But Pedro

Carneiro was with her when she left the general's compound this morning."

Diogo took a hoarse breath, closing his eyes. *Pedro*.

The trusted bodyguard who protected his wife and child. The brother of his old rival in the favela—the man who'd never forgiven him for leaving to succeed in a better world.

Diogo knew how he'd been betrayed. How the threatening notes had gotten into his home, his office, his car. *Pedro*.

A roar rose from deep in his throat as he told his security chief, "Pedro Carneiro has betrayed us. He's working for Wright. Find him and we'll find Catia—and Ellie."

But even as his body broke out into a cold sweat, he gloried in one small realization. Ellie still loved him. She'd been trying to protect them—trying to protect them all.

Diogo rose to his feet.

Protecting his family was *his* job.

Love hadn't made Diogo vulnerable. It gave him the power and strength of steel. *He would die to protect his family*.

And the baby-selling lawyer would not live to see another dawn.

CHAPTER FIFTEEN

"I DID IT," ELLIE said quietly in the dark room. "I told him I wanted a divorce because I was in love with you. Now uphold your end of the deal. Let her go."

Timothy smiled at her. His same cheerful, thin smile that he'd had for years. But everything else about him had changed. He'd once been tidy, slender and pale in wire-rimmed glasses. But he hadn't shaved for months. His clothes were dirty and baggy.

He was nearly unrecognizable, and not just in appearance. Ellie had never imagined he would hold a six-year-old girl as hostage for revenge. Looking at Catia's wide-eyed, tearstained face as the scared child clung to her teddy bear, Ellie could hardly believe that she'd once felt desperately sorry for the way she'd treated Timothy Wright.

"Nice work," he said with a satisfied nod. "I knew you just needed the right motivation to get rid of him."

Ellie looked at him with narrowed eyes. "So let the girl go."

"Sure. Fine. I never much liked kids anyway." He pushed Catia toward Pedro, who was waiting by the door. "Take her home. Or as close as you can get without being caught." Timothy turned back to Ellie with a bright, benign smile. "See? I'm not a bad person, Ellie. You've just forced me to do bad things."

Catia gave a little sob. Ellie fell to her knees in front of the girl, hugging her tight. "It's all right," she whispered, holding her close one last time. "You'll be safe. He's going to take you home." She turned fiercely to Pedro. "If you hurt her—"

"I won't. I'm just in this for the money." The man's eyes flickered at her, then Timothy. "Besides, I'm not the one you should be worried about, senhora. *Tchau*."

As they left, Ellie closed her eyes, praying for the little girl's safety. Diogo would find her. He would surely have realized by now that Ellie would never divorce him. Not when she'd told him she would love him forever…

"Alone at last," Timothy said with a sickly sweet smile.

Looking around the old concrete house with ragged curtains, tucked deeply inside the maze of the favela, Ellie felt her belly tense into another hard contraction. She'd been feeling contractions all morning. She'd felt the first one right after Diogo told her he didn't love her, and they'd only increased since Pedro had given her Timothy's note.

Now, she looked at the man she'd nearly married on that lovely spring day so long ago.

"Why did you do this?" she asked. "Why did you have me say those horrible things to Diogo?"

"I wanted him to know how it feels to lose what you love most," Timothy said, baring his teeth. "To have his heart ripped out."

"But he won't feel anything like that. He doesn't love me!"

"I've been watching you both for months. He hasn't been with another woman in all that time. Doesn't even look. He comes home every night at five sharp. You claim he's not in love? Nice try."

The thought went through her like lightning. Was it actually possible that Diogo might love her? *Oh please*, she thought, briefly closing her eyes. *Please come for me*.

Timothy gave a little cackle. "Diogo Serrador thinks he's so powerful. He's got the good looks, the charm, the billions. But I've still beaten him. *I've won you*."

She felt another contraction. A hard, long contraction that was different from the others, that made her feel weak and broke a sheen of sweat all over her body. *No*, she told the babies desperately. *Not yet*. She couldn't go into labor here!

She had to give Diogo time.

"Oh, Ellie." Sitting down on the old ragged blanket that covered the bed, Timothy looked up at her with a hangdog expression. "I love you so much, can't you see that? I would do anything for you. Ever since that day I saw you at the Dairy Burger with your blond hair glowing like an angel, I knew you were different from all the others. You never laughed at me. You respected me. Admired me. And I knew you would be mine. But you were always so worried about money. I knew I'd have to be rich for you. "

"You really did it, didn't you?" she breathed as pain went through her. "Sold babies for profit."

He shrugged. "Childless couples. Female CEOs who

spent too long on their careers. All so rich—and all so desperate for babies of their very own. While poor women give birth all the time to children they can't support. Or protect." He gave a sly grin. "I was simply providing a service. I did it for you, Ellie. Always for you."

She felt sick. How could she have missed so much of his true character? How could she have glossed over the way he'd been so obsessed with winning her? How could she have ever thought that he actually loved her?

"But Serrador ruined everything." Timothy narrowed his eyes at her belly in a way that made her fold her hands over her stomach protectively. "You'd be pregnant with my child now if not for him. I would've had you in my bed every night. Wanting me. Only me."

"No, Timothy," she said softly. She shook her head. "I made a mistake. I never should have agreed to marry you. This feeling you have for me isn't love. You don't even know me."

His thin lips turned up into a snarl.

"Perhaps you're right," he said crudely. "The girl I adored was innocent and pure. She never would have spread her legs for a Brazilian playboy like a sailor's whore."

She gasped.

Timothy shook his head and leapt up from the bed to take her arm. "I'm sorry!" he cried. "I know it was all his fault. He raped you. That's the only explanation. But do you see how love can make you do crazy things? Seeing you pregnant is driving me insane. But not for long…."

"What do you mean?" she whispered.

He gave her a cheerful smile. "I have a local doctor

on the payroll. In about an hour, he's going to help deliver your babies, and then you'll be free to come with me."

Free? The word terrified her. Another hard contraction went through her, making her knees weak. She grasped the hard metal bedframe for balance. "The babies…aren't due for two weeks," she gasped.

"It's close enough. The little brats will be fine. They'll be going to their new parents in Manhattan, who have paid me a hefty sum for newborn twins with no questions asked. I'm a rich man now, Ellie. Not as rich as Serrador, but I can buy you everything you could want. You'll never have to work again. Your only job will be to love me all day long…."

Her belly tensed, and she nearly fell. *She had to get out of here*. If she gave birth to her twins now, they would be taken from her. She and Diogo would never see them again.

She had to be strong. Strong for her children. Strong for the man she loved!

"If you take the babies, Diogo will kill you." She sat down on the bed as her legs threatened to give way beneath her.

"He won't even find me," Timothy said scornfully. "As soon as we leave here, we'll disappear forever."

She couldn't let that happen. She had to distract him. Her heart pounding, she unbuttoned the top buttons of her shirt, giving him a better look at her full cleavage. "Ooh, it's hot in here," she said, fanning herself. "Why not just let Diogo have the babies, Timothy? Then you and I can leave together."

She could see the beads of sweat on Timothy's pale, thin forehead as he came closer, staring at her chest.

"But I want Serrador to suffer," he whispered. "And those babies are my getaway money. I want that four million dollars. The private plane will take us to West Africa, to a place where he'll never find us."

She tried to hide her fear.

"What's the hurry to leave?" she said, leaning back against the bed. "Why not stay and enjoy ourselves right here?"

"Yes…" With a shudder, he buried his head in her hair, smelling it deeply. She felt him tentatively reach out to touch her breasts. It made her ill, but she forced herself to remain still.

Diogo, she thought desperately, where are you? He was so powerful, so smart. Somehow he would find them. She just had to give him time. Had to…

Timothy slowly squeezed one full breast, then the other. "Yes," he breathed. "It's so good. Just as I always thought it would be…"

But revulsion overcame Ellie. As he tried to kiss her, she couldn't stop herself from struggling. As he leaned over her, she kicked him in the face.

He fell back for a moment, dazed. But as she tried to scramble up for the door, he grabbed her hair. With a growl, he threw her back against the bed.

"So that's how it's going to be, eh?" She saw him pick up a small, wickedly gleaming knife from a tray. "Fine. Have it your way—"

She gave a desperate scream as he held the knife above her in a flash of cold steel—

A dark shadow swept upon him like an angel of death. Six feet, four inches of hard muscle threw Timothy back, tossing him to the ground.

Diogo towered over him, his expression contorted with vengeful fury.

"Serrador," he whimpered, quivering on the floor. "How?"

Diogo didn't answer. But beneath his mask of rage, Ellie saw the fear. *He'd been so afraid of losing her.*

Timothy slithered up from the floor, trying to slash at him with the knife. With a growl, Diogo punched him in the face, knocking him back down easily. He grabbed the blade, bending it back in the other man's hand. Blood trickled from Diogo's fingers, but his face showed no pain—only rage.

The knife fell to the floor with a clatter.

"Mercy. Please," Timothy cried, feebly trying to protect his face. "Don't hurt me."

"I showed you mercy. Twice." Diogo punched him across the jaw, knocking him back. "You've threatened my wife. My children. Never again!"

"Diogo," she whispered. "He didn't hurt me. Please...let him go."

"Yes, let me go!" With a high, eerie scream, Timothy fell flat onto the ground, a weak, shapeless, whimpering mass.

Diogo took a deep breath, visibly controlling his rage. "I will let you leave, Wright," he said in a low voice. "Because she asked me. But if I ever see you again..."

"You never will!"

Ellie felt another hard contraction. "Help, Diogo," she choked. "The babies…"

Diogo immediately flew to her. He fell on his knees before the bed, cradling her face in his arms. "Ellie. What's wrong?"

"Catia?" she gasped. "Did you—find—"

"She's safe," he said. "We have her. We found Pedro. But if Wright hurt you—"

"I'm all right," she sobbed, holding him tight. "But I'm having contractions. The babies are coming."

He picked her up in his strong arms.

"You're safe now, *querida,*" he said soothingly. "My bodyguards are right behind me. We'll get you to the hospital."

Ellie caressed his strong, handsome face.

"You came for me," she whispered in wonder. "You knew I would never leave you. You know I'll love you forever."

"I knew." Unshed tears shone in his dark eyes as he shook his head. "It just took me too damned long. Forgive me for being a coward and a fool." He looked down at her. "I love you, Ellie. Your strength, your pure heart, your joy. I want you to know. I will love you until the day I die."

He loved her.

A rush of joy went through her body.

But she saw Timothy rise to his knees behind them. Holding a gun in his hand, he raised it deliberately…

"Diogo!" she shrieked. "Look out!"

Diogo turned, holding heavily pregnant Ellie in his arms. But he moved slowly. Too slowly.

Timothy said hoarsely, "If I can't have her..."

And he fired.

EPILOGUE

"OH, MOM, LOOK! SNOW!"

Christmas morning dawned bright and fine. Snow had fallen overnight in New York. Ellie looked up from the quiet hush of the front room sofa, where she'd been nursing one of her six-week-old babies while the other one slept in a little bassinet beside her. The house was unusually dark and quiet. The servants had the day off. Ellie had been dreaming, watching the twinkling blue lights of the enormous Christmas tree when she heard Catia—now officially her adopted daughter—clap her hands with delight.

"Can we go outside, Mom?" the little girl pleaded, wiggling in front of the large plate window as only an ecstatic six-year-old could. "Please, can we?"

"It's Christmas morning!" Ellie replied with a soft laugh. "Don't you want to open your presents?"

Catia spared a quick glance over at the tree, and for an instant seemed to waver. "Yes, but…" She glanced back at the window. "I've never seen snow before!"

Ellie heard a creak on the stairs. She loved all the creaks of this one-hundred-year-old house. Especially when she recognized the footsteps.

"Diogo," she said. A glow went through her as he entered the room. Even dressed in a white T-shirt and pajama pants, with his chin dark with bristle and his hair a mess, he was the handsomest man in the world to her.

"Ellie." His dark eyes lit up with his smile as he came down the stairs. On the other side of the sofa, he leaned over to kiss Ellie on the lips. *"Feliz Natal, meu amor."*

"Merry Christmas," she replied, caressing his cheek.

"Papa?" Catia cried eagerly. "Can we go play in the snow?"

Diogo groaned, stretching with a yawn. "Just a minute, little one."

Ellie grinned impishly at the dark circles under his eyes. "Thanks for keeping Gabriel company last night."

He grinned back, glancing down at the baby snuggled in her arms. "I wouldn't miss it."

Life was a miracle, she thought happily. Since Diogo told her he loved her, every day was a new precious miracle to her.

In more ways than one. When Timothy had raised the gun in the favela, she'd thought their lives were over. She'd felt Diogo whirl around to protect her and the unborn twins with the shield of his body. But when the team of bodyguards stormed into the concrete house, he'd given a final frustrated scream—and turned the gun on himself.

The babies had arrived in Diogo's Bentley on the way to the hospital. In spite of the many potential complications of a multiple birth—particularly being born in the backseat of a car—both Ana and Gabriel were healthy and thriving. Another gift to be grateful for, in this bright Christmas season....

Christmas in New York. Three weeks ago, Diogo had bought Ellie this historic nine-bedroom mansion. With a backyard—extremely rare for the Upper East Side—and a rooftop garden with a view of Central Park, the house was a showplace that had cost nearly fifty million dollars.

No, Diogo didn't fool around when it came to giving presents, she thought wryly.

Every day, he found some new way of making her happy. He didn't realize that just having him love her and the children was the greatest gift of all.

"Where's Ana?" Diogo asked.

"Sleeping in her bassinet."

"Lucky baby." With another yawn, Diogo went to pour himself some coffee in the kitchen. He'd been up with his son for most of the night. Gabriel only seemed interested in night sleeping if his father held him against his chest, walking him up and down the creaking hallways.

Ellie glanced fondly at baby Ana, sleeping soundly in the bassinet. She was a much better sleeper than her brother—perhaps because Ana was more mature. After all, she was older by four minutes.

"Papa!" Catia begged, jumping up and down in agony. She'd already put on her coat over her pajamas and boots on her bare feet.

"I can help you, kiddo," Lilibeth said as she came down the stairs. "I can show how to make a snowman. I'm a pro. Just let me put on my lipstick."

"Lipstick?" Ellie exclaimed. "Who do you expect to meet in the backyard?"

"A woman never knows where she'll find her

prince," Lilibeth said airily. "But I'm only free until New Year's Eve. Harold Wynn is taking me out to the Flint Factory Ball!"

Ellie repressed a smile. Lilibeth had really come into her own since they'd returned to the U.S. But she insisted on keeping her own home in Flint, though she often spent weekends in New York visiting her grandchildren and shopping on Fifth Avenue. She'd become queen of her own town, driving all over in her yellow Ferrari, hosting Diogo at her house when he'd come to negotiate to buy the old factory.

He'd created a new subsidiary to sell specialty metals abroad, and decided Flint was the perfect location for the factory. As Ellie had been unwilling to travel much since the babies were born, Lilibeth had become his de facto hostess. She'd recently bought the biggest mansion on Main Street—the house that had gone on the market after Timothy Wright's shocking suicide.

"I never liked that man," Lilibeth had told her gravely when she learned of his baby-selling business. "I told you all along to wait for your true love, Ellie. Aren't you glad you listened to me!"

Ellie's smile faded. She still felt troubled when she remembered how Timothy had shot himself that horrible day in the favela. And yet, she admitted quietly to herself, she was glad to know that he would never threaten her family again, or try to steal another woman's baby for his own profit.

Snuggling her son a little closer, she watched her grandmother, now chic in her signature bright orange lipstick and wearing a black puffy coat, run outside to play with Catia in the snow.

"Papa, you have to come, too!" the little girl insisted, pausing at the door. "Come now!" she ordered, every bit as bossy as her father. Then she ran into the backyard to play.

Diogo stared after her ruefully then shook his head. "I guess I have to go play in the snow." He sighed. "Unless you need me?" he added hopefully.

She smiled at him, loving him with all her heart. "I always need you. But at the moment, I think Catia needs you more." Ellie looked down at the hungry baby making contented gulps against her breast. His eyes were closed and he slept drowsily as she stroked his soft, downy hair. "Your son will keep me busy for some time."

For several moments, they both looked down at their babies.

"Thank you for the best Christmas gift any man has ever had." Diogo's dark eyes met hers. "I love you, Ellie."

She opened her mouth to reply, but he stopped her with a light kiss that soon deepened into something far more provocative.

He looked down at her wickedly, quirking an eyebrow. "I'll give you your Christmas present later."

"Another present? You already gave me this house!"

"I have something else in mind." By the hungry look in his face, she knew exactly what he meant to give her, and she shivered. Her heart started to pound. It had been so long since they'd last made love. They'd been so busy since the babies were born....

"As soon as they're asleep, you're mine," he whispered. Reaching into the hall closet, he tossed his black cashmere coat over his T-shirt then paused at the door, looking at her. "I've always wanted to make love to a woman wearing nothing but a hundred-carat diamond necklace."

"But I don't have—"

"You haven't seen what's under the tree," he said mischievously, and scampered outside.

Watching her grandmother and husband and daughter throw snowballs at each other through the back window, Ellie realized she'd never been so happy. She glanced at her two sleeping babies. She'd never dreamed life could be like this. Fate had created a life far better than she'd ever imagined for herself.

Fate, and Diogo.

"I love you, too," she whispered aloud, and as she heard the soft whistle of the wind and the warm sigh of slumbering babies, she blessed the day that her boss had first seduced her in Rio.

Meet the Buchanan dynasty – where secrets are about to be revealed…

Delicious

The billionaire tycoon and the cook!

Available 6th March 2009

Irresistible

The sexy soldier and the single mum!

Available 4th September 2009

FREE!
4 Books
and a surprise gift!

We would like to take this opportunity to thank you for reading this Mills & Boon® book by offering you the chance to take FOUR more specially selected titles from the Modern™ series absolutely FREE! We're also making this offer to introduce you to the benefits of the Mills & Boon® Book Club™—

- ★ FREE home delivery
- ★ FREE gifts and competitions
- ★ FREE monthly Newsletter
- ★ Exclusive Mills & Boon Book Club offers
- ★ Books available before they're in the shops

Accepting these FREE books and gift places you under no obligation to buy. you may cancel at any time. even after receiving your free shipment. Simply complete your details below and return the entire page to the address below. You don't even need a stamp!

YES! Please send me 4 free Modern books and a surprise gift. I understand that unless you hear from me. I will receive 6 superb new titles every month for just £3.19 each. postage and packing free. I am under no obligation to purchase any books and may cancel my subscription at any time. The free books and gift will be mine to keep in any case.

P9ZEF

Ms/Mrs/Miss/Mr ....Initials..................................
BLOCK CAPITALS PLEASE
Surname ....
Address...
....
....Postcode.....................................

Send this whole page to:
UK: FREEPOST CN81, Croydon, CR9 3WZ